ROD'S GIRL

ROD'S GIRL

by Harriett H. Carr

Hastings House, Publishers

New York

TO ELEANOR STEELE LITTLE,

my friend since our high school days.

Published simultaneously in Canada
by S. J. Reginald Saunders, Publishers, Toronto 2B.

Library of Congress Catalog Card Number: 63-16166
Printed in the United States of America

Junior Literary Guild 1963

CONTENTS

5

CHAPTER I

SLICK PAVEMENT

MARGE RAGLAND stood on the top step of the Andover City auditorium and surveyed the wet sidewalk and trees dripping in the misty night. It had stopped raining so she wouldn't need to pull out the blue plastic boots now folded tightly in a bag that was part of her new rain outfit. She stuffed the Summer Drama Festival program in her coat pocket and pulled the rain cap over her light brown curls. Such short curls. She had to keep her hair cut that way because it wouldn't lie in lovely shoulder-length waves like her older sister Janey's copper colored hair. Just a step ahead, Bill Tanner was helping Janey with her rain coat.

"Okay, we'll be seeing you," her sister called back to her, and Bill echoed a "See you," as the two started down the steps.

Marge didn't like being a lonesome third in the Tanner car, so she had told them she would ride home with some of the other students from Eastfield. Bill never had much to say to

Marge. He had been coaxing Janey to go steady all summer, and Marge was sure he would be glad if her younger sister went home another way. At intermission, however, everyone had been talking at once and Marge hadn't made any arrangements for a ride. Janey and Bill didn't know that, and now she was left alone.

Marge turned back to the emptying auditorium. She didn't see anyone from Eastfield among the people hurrying out to their cars. It was a little frightening now, but at the same time there was a feeling of independence and exhilaration in being miles from home alone at eleven o'clock at night—a sense of being grown-up that she hadn't experienced very often in her fifteen years.

Marge knew there was a bus, but she wasn't sure of the time schedule or the fare. The Raglands always drove between Eastfield, where Dr. Ragland was president of a small college, and Andover City. She thought she had plenty of money, but she decided to look around the parking lot anyway. Perhaps she would see an Eastfield car there.

The big square of wet pavement glistened, reflecting neon signs and automobile lights in shimmering ripples. Marge waited on the sidewalk until the last car had splashed past her onto the street, then she started for the bus station. It would be fun riding home in the night with travelers she didn't know. No one would expect anything special of her because she was Dr. Ragland's daughter, and Janey wouldn't be there planning everything and telling her what to do. It wasn't that Janey was ever disagreeable; just always right and always with a better idea than Marge ever had. Janey was a leader—the kind of daughter a college president should have.

Marge had been past the bus station but never inside before, and she hesitated in the doorway. Ticket windows half covered by black iron grills, telephone booths and rest rooms lined one wall. A lunch counter with a green top extended the length of the opposite side of the building. Between were rows of dark oak benches on which sat weary looking women with packages and suitcases, and men blowing tobacco smoke. She walked to the nearest ticket window.

"When is the next bus to Eastfield?" she asked.

"You just missed one," an elderly ticket agent replied, peering at her over his glasses. "Busses run every hour on the hour up to midnight. Next after that will be at six in the morning."

Midnight! What would Mother and Dad say? Why had she been so eager to get away from Janey and Bill?

"How much is the fare?" She hoped her voice didn't betray the alarm she felt now.

"Eighty-five cents."

Marge opened her rain bag and immediately panicked. She didn't have eighty-five cents. She had forgotten about the chocolate milk shake she had bought that afternoon!

Someone stepped into line behind her and coughed with annoyance. Marge took a time schedule from a metal holder and walked to the door.

What was she to do? Phone Mother, of course. Mother would drive over and get her. Or she might know someone in Andover City who could let her have some money. Only how she dreaded to explain this latest misadventure to her father!

She looked up and down the drab street, now almost empty of cars as well as people. If only someone from Eastfield would come along!

"Beep-beep! Beep-beep!"

Marge almost jumped. She knew that old auto horn. Rodney Maguire was in some of her classes at school, but he hadn't been in Andover City for the Drama Festival, she was sure. And she wasn't sure Mother and Dad would want her to ride home with him. "Hot Rod Maguire" had been his nickname ever since he raced an Andover City student all the way between the two towns after a basketball game last year. He had won, but nobody thought it was very smart, even though the other student had been wrong in trying to crowd ahead of Rod when they left the school parking lot. But now . . . tonight . . .

"Hi, Marge! Want a lift home?"

"I certainly do," she answered and hurried toward the car. It was then she realized Rod wasn't alone. A boy she had never seen before turned lazily in the front seat and opened the back door for her. He wasn't getting out of the car to do it as Bill Tanner would have done, but most of the boys at school weren't as formal as Bill. Worse than that, he wasn't making her one of them by having her crowd into the front seat, which she would have preferred.

"Jerome Chamberlin," Rod said by way of introduction. "Jerry's new in Eastfield. Comes from here—Andover City. He isn't sure he likes us."

Marge couldn't get much of an impression of Jerry as the car started. Dark hair, slicked back as the boys were beginning to wear it; full features, broad shoulders. She was conscious of the openly appraising look he gave her.

"Oh, it wouldn't be too hard to like some people, I guess," he said. He probably meant it as a compliment, but she wasn't sure she liked the way he said it.

"How come you're here, in the middle of the night, practically?" Rod asked as the car slid away from the bus station. "Did you get stood up, or did you have to teach somebody a lesson?"

Marge's cheeks flushed and she was glad for the darkness of the back seat. She knew Rod was teasing, but how was she to answer? Explain the situation? Laugh it off?

"Ignore him," Jerry said without turning around. "That's what I always do." It sounded as though the boys had been friends for some time. Who was Jerome Chamberlin?

"Your sense of humor, Rod!" Marge tried to tease back. "It's really . . ."

"Sinister is the word," Rod laughed. "But aren't you risking your life, riding with an obnoxious character who's known to have driven more than thirty-five miles an hour, and who's been ticketed for parking next to a fire hydrant, and who wasn't attending your highbrow Summer Drama Festival. Informed though. I know where you've been."

That was another thing about Rodney. His uncle, "Shorty" Maguire, was a reporter and columnist for the *Eastfield Clarion* and seemed to have listening posts in every block. Some of Shorty's cock-sureness and cynicism must have rubbed off on Rod. He was built like Shorty too; thin and angular, hollow-cheeked, questioning brown eyes and unruly brown hair. But there was something about him that had always made Marge think she would like him if she knew him better.

"What was the play about, Marge?" he asked.

"You might have liked it," she answered. "It wasn't the usual Shakespeare. Because it was the last play of the season it was a new one for us. 'The World We Want.'"

"H-m-m-m-m! The world I want won't ever be on this town's stage," Rod snorted. "I wish we didn't have to go to Andover City every time we want to see a good show or shoot a game of pool, or bowl. It gets me to have to go there for everything, and have them look at you as though you were the country cousin."

"Nobody was looking 'country' at you after that double tonight," Jerry told him and there was admiration in the remark. "You've been doing real good for almost a year now." Plainly Rod was pleased.

"I wish somebody had been offering a buck a pin," he answered.

The boys seemed ready to leave Marge out of the conversation and she didn't want to be left out. This year Marge hoped some boy would ask her for regular dates. A movie in Andover City, a dance at the Country Club there, chop suey afterwards or a spaghetti supper—that was the social pattern. Marge was starting her sophomore year next week. Except for her hair she knew she was almost as pretty as Janey. They had the same deep blue eyes and long, dark lashes. She wished someone would really notice her this year. It probably shouldn't be Rod. Dad would think he didn't compare with Bill Tanner. Who was this Jerome Chamberlin?

"Do girls ever bowl?" She asked, leaning forward in the back seat.

"Tut-tut! Mustn't use naughty words," Rod chided. "Suppose somebody heard Dr. Ragland's daughter asking about bowling!"

"Dr. Ragland's daughter?" Jerry repeated, and turned to look at her once more as they passed under the next street light. "VIP's? I always wanted to meet one."

His tone said he didn't; that he resented important people. He shifted back in the front seat and she couldn't see his face. No, Jerome wouldn't be the boy to date her. It wasn't because she felt important. It was her lack of any such potential that bothered her most of the time. But from the hint of hostility in his voice, she felt it would be difficult to get along with Jerome.

Marge didn't really mind Rod's kidding and she understood his resentment. "Andover City's dormitory," Shorty had called it in one of his stinging barbs. A town that was more and more overcrowded with people who worked and shopped and had their good times somewhere else.

Marge tried to think of something to say to keep the conversation going.

"What did you sign up for beside the regular required schedule, Rod?" she asked. Then, by way of explanation to Jerry, "They had us do a pre-registration at school last spring, so they would know what fall enrollment would be, and what new courses we'd like. I guess what's most in demand is what we'll get."

"Think so?" Rod asked. "I signed up for electronics, but we'll not get it. What were you dreaming about when you filled out that form?"

"Plastics," Marge told him. "I got Carol and Lois to sign up too. What makes you think we won't get what we asked for?"

"Money," Rod answered dryly, "Any new course costs money. And the money-men in this town don't care what we kids want."

That was a point Marge had not considered. Her father hadn't seemed to think much of her idea when she had told him what she had done, but he hadn't opposed it. It was important to Marge though. She was sure she could make beautiful things with plastics if there was a course to teach her how.

The boys had stopped talking. Highway Four stretched ahead like a sliver of silver in the wet August night. No star blinked above them, not a light gleamed in the farm houses that slid past. Marge was afraid Rodney was driving too fast, but he was slowing for the curves, keeping to the right side of the two-way macadam strip when they came to each hill. The road from Andover City to Eastfield wound through gently rolling farmland. It was a pretty, tree-shaded road in the daytime. Nearing midnight, it was a closed-in, lonely road and only two cars were in sight now, red taillights of a passenger car ahead, bright headlights of a truck coming toward them. Marge felt the car slowing down and was relieved that Rod wasn't trying to pass the car ahead before the truck had gone by. She didn't sense the nearness of the car nor realize what was happening until she heard Rod's horrified gasp.

He had swung to the right shoulder of the road and Marge had only seconds in which to glimpse the auto just ahead, to feel Rod's car sliding on the wet pavement and down the embankment, to hear the screech of brakes and the honk of Rod's horn as his arm pressed against the wheel. Then noise and movement ended and she waited, expecting to feel pain or to black out. Nothing happened. The engine's hum was silenced. Dripping leaves on an over-hanging tree glistened in the up-shot headlights. She had been jammed against the side of the tilted car and could no longer see the road.

"Are you all right, Marge?" Rod sounded frightened. "What about you, Jerry?"

"I'm all right," Marge answered. Her feet were higher than

13

her head and she was afraid to move, but she didn't think she was hurt. "What about you?"

She could hear Rod fumbling with the car door. "Okay. We can get out this way."

Righting herself, she saw him crawling under the wheel, Jerry following.

"Hey," a man's voice called from the road above. "Anybody hurt?"

"I don't think so," Rod replied, opening the back door to help Marge climb out and jump to the solid earth below her. The man reached a firm hand down and pulled her up the embankment. He was dressed in coveralls and Marge could guess he was the truck driver. He was a large, broad-shouldered man, almost a head taller than Jerry, the larger of the two boys.

From the road ahead came other voices and to Marge, sickening recognition. It was Janey and Bill and they would tell her father! She couldn't ask them not to.

"Is anyone hurt?" That was Janey.

"What happened?" Bill called out. Then an astonished "Marge!" from both of them. She was grateful they didn't begin to question her right away.

"How did it happen?" Bill repeated, speaking directly to Rodney. In the gleaming headlights Marge saw the frown between his gray eyes and the worried look on his serious face. "Gee, Rod, the road is straight along here. And my taillights are on." He sounded anxious to be cleared of any responsibility.

"I was being careless, of course," Rod said irritably. "Reckless, teen-age driver!"

"Take it easy," the truck driver said. "Got your driver's license? How old are you?"

Rodney pulled a wallet from the hip pocket of his bluejeans and handed his student license to the driver. "I'm sixteen," he said. "Everything's in order."

"Whose car is it?"

"Are you the State Police or something?" Rodney demanded. "It's my uncle's car. Shorty Maguire. Douglas Maguire, that is. He works for the town paper. Ask any of these kids."

"You're getting kind of bothered, aren't you?" the man asked. "I don't have to help you out of the ditch. It just happens the company I work for expects it of us drivers. We're expected to make a report, too."

"He's telling the truth," Janey spoke up at once. "We're all students at Eastfield High School. At least four of us are. And this is Shorty's car all right."

"Maybe your uncle's likely to be sore," the driver suggested. Then, to Bill, "Drive ahead a little and wait. I'll see what I can do."

"Marge, you come with us," Janey directed. "Girls are just in the way here."

"If you can't get Rod's car out of the ditch, we can get everyone home," Bill offered. "Janey, do you want to move our car? Maybe I can help here."

In the light from the overturned car, Janey's hair was shining. She drew her dark green rain coat tighter around her neat little figure and her high heels clicked a self-assured rat-tat-tat as she led the way to Bill's car, Marge following. Janey drove it ahead and pulled to the side. Turning in the front seat, the girls watched while the truck driver fastened a chain to Rodney's car and eased it up onto the highway.

"What happened?" Janey asked. "Was Rod at the Drama Festival? Who is this other boy? I never saw him before."

As briefly as she could, Marge explained. Then Bill came back to the car and Jerry with him, while Rod remained with his righted automobile. The truck driver was turning the engine off and on and apparently testing the car for safety before he let Rod have the wheel again.

"Rod wants to be sure Marge is all right," Jerry explained. He was looking at Janey now, in the same way he had looked at Marge earlier in the evening. "Rod's car is okay, but maybe you'd better keep an eye on us in your rear view mirror, just in case."

"Of course we will," Janey promised at once. "And Marge is fine. Not even as frightened as I'd have been."

Marge had not been frightened at all. There hadn't been time to be frightened. "I'm all right," Marge said quickly. "Thank Rod for picking me up."

"That's okay," Jerry said. "Maybe you'll get a chance to make a strike yourself, some day. So long now."

"What did he mean about making a strike?" Janey asked as soon as he was gone.

"We'd been talking about Rod's good bowling, and how we have to go to Andover for just about everything," Marge explained. "I was wishing there was some place for girls to bowl, here at home."

"Going to Andover City gives us something to do," Bill said. "I don't mind."

"I know what you mean, though," Janey agreed. Her voice was dreamy and she was leaning against Bill's shoulder gently.

Marge didn't think either Janey or Bill really knew what she meant. They both would be away next year, Bill at Harvard and Janey at Skidmore, a college where girls could elect to spend their third year abroad. The future was so glamorous for both of them. Marge was the one who would stay in Eastfield. She and Rod and probably Jerome.

Bill stopped the car in the driveway beside the Ragland's store and stucco house and waited for Marge to leave. Mother and Dad didn't object to their sitting in the side yard for a little while, so long as they did not drive to the town's Lover's Lane, a wooded section of the old Dodd estate along the river, which Eastfield could not afford to keep up as a part of Dodd Park.

Marge walked across the lawn to the front door, surveying the windows apprehensively. A bright light in the den at the back of the house meant that Dad was working, and that Marge might as well tell him now and get it over with.

She stood in the wide hall beside the winding stairway trying to think of the words to say. It was awful to have your father disappointed in you, especially when he was such a fine man, and prominent throughout the state. Marge hadn't thought of him as anyone other than just Daddy—a short, plumpish man who played with her when he could get the time—until she had reached Junior High School. Gradually she had come to realize there were standards Dr. Ragland's family should maintain, and she hadn't been fully equal to them. Painful memories of poor grades in math came back to her now. Janey was an all-A student, a leader in club activities and quick with everything. Janey measured up, and she never got into situations like this one.

Nervously Marge rapped on the study door and waited until her father called to her to come in. His desk was heaped with architect's drawings and he looked up from the load of work to smile wearily. He seemed shorter and more tired than usual behind that big desk. How she hated to add to his anxieties now.

"Home, Marge?" Then his smile vanished. Her expression must have warned him that something was wrong. "What's the matter?" he asked.

The desk light glistened on her father's rumpled, thinning brown hair, and the short brush of moustache that was beginning to turn gray. His eyes were deep set with worry lines showing beneath them, and the lines in his forehead tightened while he waited for her to answer.

"It isn't anything very bad, only I've got to tell you," Marge began trying to keep a quiver out of her voice.

He motioned her to a chair. "Well, sit down, dear. What is it?"

"It was an accident, but nobody was hurt. Not even the car. I was riding home from the Drama Festival with Rodney Maguire and a friend of his and we slid into the ditch. Bill and Janey were right there and they brought me home."

She stood just inside the door and said it as fast as she could.

17

Dr. Ragland looked at the work on his desk for a second, then pushed the papers aside with a sigh.

"Sit down," he repeated. "Now tell me exactly what happened, and why you were with Rodney. You went with Janey and Bill."

Marge told him everything. It wasn't easy, especially explaining why she hadn't wanted to ride home with her sister. That was the thing Dad seemed to understand best.

"But when you didn't have another ride, why did you let Janey and Bill go on without you? Suppose there wasn't a bus at that hour of night?" he asked.

"I've heard busses coming down Main Street all night, I think." It was a whisper.

"I'm not sure they stop in Eastfield," her father said. "The through, over-night busses don't. Did you think of that?"

"I guess I didn't."

"What would you have done if there hadn't been a bus until morning, and the boys hadn't happened along?" he pressed.

"I'd have phoned Mother." Her voice was barely audible. She couldn't tell him she was about to make that phone call when Rodney saw her.

Her father didn't speak for a few minutes. When he did, his words were a reprimand.

"Marge, you're old enough to think things through better than this. So you'd have called Mother. Of course we would have come for you, but I couldn't have let your mother make the trip alone, around midnight. I'd have had to leave my work and go too. I'm studying these architects' plans so I can make a good report to the state officials, and I'm pressed for time. Did you think of that?"

Marge shook her head. She couldn't trust her voice now.

"After you'd let Janey leave you, and you were at the bus station alone, it would have been difficult for you to refuse a ride home with your school friends, of course," he went on. "But isn't Rodney the boy who was in some scrape last year?"

Marge wanted to say it wasn't a scrape, really. Almost any

boy would have done what Rod did. But she couldn't explain it to her father now.

"Wasn't he the one who was in some reckless driving escapade?" he pressed.

She could only nod, miserably.

"This could have been a serious accident," her father went on. "If Rod had smashed into Bill's car I shudder to think where you all might be now."

He walked to the window and adjusted the blinds, leaving Marge to think about his words. It could have been a bad accident, he was right. She stared at his stooped shoulders until he turned back to her.

"Marge, there isn't anything to do about it now but be thankful." He wasn't smiling. "But I don't want you riding anywhere with Rodney again until I've met him. I don't want to misjudge him, but until I have a chance to talk to him you're not to get into any car he's driving."

She nodded once more, but what could she say to Rod if he asked her again? It would be the last time if she refused.

"And Marge, do try to think of outcomes before you jump into things," she heard her father cautioning. "A girl of fifteen should be developing judgment."

He was right, she knew. She hadn't even realized until now how narrowly she had escaped a serious accident. She stared at the worn oriental rug and wished he would say she was forgiven, but he didn't say anything more. He had turned away and was staring out of the window, off in the direction of his college on the hill, which he couldn't see in the darkness of night.

"I'm sorry, Dad."

"Well, I'm glad you're safely home," he told her. "Now get to bed, for it's late."

She went into the hall, closing the door quietly behind her. She wouldn't have minded if he had scolded her harder, if he had only seemed to understand.

CHAPTER II

PLATOON SYSTEM

Shorty Maguire wrote a column for *The Clarion*, East-field's only paper, which he called "In Short." Marge as well as everyone else knew who wrote it. Bits of gossip that weren't really news, news without names because important people didn't want the items printed at all, and occasionally one of Shorty's own editorial ideas in a caustic capsule—that was the column. It was read with more relish than the pompous editorials the owner, Judson Whiting, wrote. Mr. Whiting seemed always to be trying to impress people.

Marge was raking leaves Saturday afternoon while Mother and her neighbor, Mrs. Brundage, were on the porch discussing fall gardening when the newsboy hurled the paper against the Ragland's front steps. It ricocheted into the yard, landing at Marge's feet and she stopped her work to sit on the steps and read it. She had never expected "to make" Shorty's column, but she knew before she had finished the first sentence what his lead story was about. The item was headed "Lightning Strikes Thrice."

"Taking a car without permission of the owner is just borrowing when it's in the family, so this case will never appear on the municipal court docket. Besides, the two teen-age boys involved have been punished enough, and the girl was really an innocent by-stander waiting for the bus when the boys drove along.

"Hurrying home after a trip to Andover City the driver (guiltiest of the two) tried to slow down too quickly on the wet pavement. Result, the car slid down an embankment on Highway Four with some minor damage which he will have to pay for. (Strike one.) Home after the established deadlines, the boys tried rear-window entrances to avoid time checks and questionings. One fell from a second story porch roof and broke his wrist. (Strike two.) The other, whose family has just moved to Eastfield, stumbled on an assortment of barrels and boxes, brought the china cabinet down on his luckless heels in a family-rousing ruin. (Strike three.) The third member of the party got home without mishap which is as it should be, for she is a nice girl. Our kindest advice: take the bus next time."

Marge could scarcely believe what she was reading. That the boys should have had more trouble after the accident was almost too much. It was Jerome whose family had just moved to Eastfield, so it must be Rodney who had suffered the broken wrist. She winced at the thought of the pain he must have suffered. A broken wrist would interfere with his after-school job at *The Clarion*. He was the one who counted out papers for the newsboys and carried the business route, coming up Main Street to Jewett Avenue where she lived.

This publicity in Shorty's column was the last thing Marge desired. What was her father going to say about it? Shorty didn't have to mention names. Everybody would know the story when Rodney appeared with an arm in a sling. Someone would tell who the girl was, of course. She dreaded to face her father tonight, and she could imagine the whole school buzzing next week.

Marge sat on the steps holding the paper as inconspicuously as possible until Mrs. Brundage left, then she took it to her mother.

"Now I have disgraced you," Marge said, opening the paper to the "In Short" column.

During her years as the wife of a college dean and later a

college president, her mother had learned to understand problems and to see all sides of every question. She never annoyed anyone needlessly or appeared upset. Her light brown, waving hair and quiet ways were Marge's inheritance, and Marge had been given her mother's good, reliable name, too. But Mother had a spark Marge could not recognize in herself. She raised her eyebrows questioningly now and took the paper.

Marge stared after Mrs. Brundage, who was disappearing down Jewett Avenue. Mrs. Brundage was as unchanging as a monument. She went to the beauty parlor once a week, but she kept her fading blond hair in the old-fashioned straight bob that must have been the fashion thirty years ago when she was young. She went to New York for new clothes twice a year, but her tailored suits and dresses always looked the same. With all her money she could afford to ignore fashions, Janey had explained with a sigh.

Mrs. Brundage lived in the largest house on tree-shaded Jewett Avenue and she had two automobiles. Her husband owned the major automobile agency in Eastfield, and the best combination garage and second-hand car lot too. The mechanics who didn't work for him just eked out a living in small repair shops near the gasoline stations. Besides that Mrs. Brundage's brother was Alexander Dodd, Jr., president of the bank. It was their father who had given Dodd Park to Eastfield, and the marshy acres beyond it down by the river. What was she going to say when she read that little item?

"It must be Rodney who has the broken wrist," Mother commented, and she shuddered too.

Marge nodded. "I didn't know anything about that part of it until just now." She wiped her perspiring hands on her soiled dark blue shorts. "What's Dad going to say?"

"I guess he'll think we can live it down," Mother said with a reassuring smile. "Shorty probably thought he had to print something about it, or people would accuse him of suppressing news when it involves his own nephew."

"But what am I going to say at school?" Marge wailed. "The kids will all be asking questions and Rodney will tell them I'm the girl who was with Jerry and him."

"So what?" Mother asked. "It was nothing serious except for the later misfortunes. You weren't doing anything to be ashamed of, so why be embarrassed about it?"

Marge shook her head dolefully and went back to the rustling leaves. It would be easy for Mother or Janey to carry it off, but she was going to feel uncomfortable when Carol and Lois Simmons, her particular friends, questioned her.

Monday morning she dressed in her new two-tone blue sweater and skirt for the first day at school. She thought it was prettier than the subdued red-rust sweater and hunter green skirt Janey had selected, but even so Janey appeared more gay and alive than she did when they started down the walk.

The main corridor was crowded as Marge had never seen it before when they arrived. Boys and girls jammed in front of the four large bulletin boards where schedules were posted for freshmen, sophomores, juniors and seniors. Janey left Marge to join her own class as soon as they reached the sophomore board, and for a moment Marge stood alone, surveying the old school hall. The walls had been given another coat of drab green paint during the summer, but the place still looked dingy and smelled of chalk dust.

It was only seconds before Carol and Lois were clutching at her arms.

"You of all people," Carol laughed, a little too loudly. Her flaming red outfit and her quick gestures would have attracted attention if she hadn't said anything.

"Which one did you have the date with?" Lois whispered. "Rod, I hope. He's so exciting. I don't know this new boy, of course." She was looking up and down the corridors, appraising all the newcomers. "But Rod Maguire!"

"How did you find out I was the girl?" Marge asked, pleasantly surprised to find herself the center of favorable attention when she had feared condemnation. Several other girls were looking at her and smiling as though they would like to be included in the conversation. She hadn't expected anyone to envy her the experience.

"We saw Rodney on Sunday—wrist bandaged and arm in a sling," Carol announced, again loudly enough for her voice to carry above the din. "Wait until you see him. Or have you? Have things been shaping up in Eastfield while we were at the lake?"

Carol's bright black eyes were darting from one group to another. She was a small, eager girl anxious not to miss anything. Marge didn't answer her.

"What's new on the bulletin board?" Marge asked instead. "I can't see the bottom of it for the crowd. Where did all these kids come from?"

"I don't know," Carol answered. "A lot more new families must have moved to town this summer. There isn't anything new on the schedule except the social studies teacher and we knew he was coming. His name is Dr. Tozian and he's from Cleveland. His wife's sick and needs to be out of doors a lot and in a quiet place. That's how we got him in Eastfield, I guess."

"No plastics, then?" Marge asked. She supposed she was prepared for it. She and Carol and Lois had decided to ask for the course after they had read a newspaper story about a girl who was paying her way through college by making plastic novelties. She had learned the skill in a high school vocational course, so Marge had taken the article to Mr. Matthews' industrial arts department last spring. He was always approachable and had been so interested that Marge had really hoped something would be done. Now it appeared Rodney had been right.

"Maybe we could start a new club and do something after school," Marge suggested.

"How?" Carol asked. "I wouldn't know how to start to begin!"

24

"Mr. Matthews would know," Marge assured her. "We could ask him and find out."

They started down the hall. At the junior bulletin board they met Rod, arm in a sling, and the new boy Jerome. At Eastfield High School, frosh and sophomore boys wore bluejeans, juniors and seniors wore slacks and shirts or jackets. Jerome, obviously a junior hadn't known or hadn't conformed anyway. He stood with his hands in the back pockets of his bluejeans, ill at ease and unfriendly, when Rod introduced him to the boys and girls who would be his classmates.

"You look like good football material," Bill Tanner said in an effort to welcome the newcomer. "We can use you."

"Not me," Jerry said. "Somebody's got to take Rod's place at *The Clarion*." He turned from Bill to the bulletin board. "Haven't they got anything except English and math and stuff like that? No shops except woodworking and printing?"

Bill hesitated before answering. Jerome was not making a good impression and Marge wondered at the friendship which seemed to have developed between Rod and him.

"We've got good equipment in the science labs," Bill said at last. "We aren't behind in the important things. And we have a new social studies teacher. . . ."

"And English and math and languages," Jerome interrupted. "I can see."

Uncomfortably Marge turned to Rod. "Maybe you can help Carol and me. You took printing from Mr. Matthews. We thought he might sponsor a plastic club, only we don't know enough about it to ask an intelligent question."

"Sophomores aren't supposed to have minds yet," Rod grinned. He wasn't looking at Jerome but his unresponsive new friend was obviously on his mind. "Mr. Matthews can help Jerry, anyway. The boys really turn out keen work in his woodworking courses. All who want to see Mr. Matthews meet me here after school. Okay?" He brushed his rumpled brown hair off his high forehead with a self-conscious gesture that was not like Rodney Maguire.

"Good enough," Carol agreed as the first bell sounded, and Marge nodded in agreement.

When she reached her first class, she stopped in astonishment. There were more students than seats, and it was the same in the next class and the next. Students stood along the walls while teachers had the newcomers fill out enrollment slips as the others had done in the spring pre-school registration.

Marge had scheduled social studies after lunch. It was the first class where she and Rodney had been near each other in the overflowing rooms, and the first time she had been able to say a personal word to him.

"Does it still hurt?" she asked, with a gesture toward his bandaged arm.

Rodney shook his head. "It was A *Night*, wasn't it?" he asked quietly. "And this is going to be *The Class*. Have you heard about this guy?" He lowered his voice and stepped nearer to her.

"You mean Dr. Tozian?" Marge turned her head away from the young instructor.

"None other. He's going to organize a High School Chamber of Commerce. Each class is to select two delegates. We get a week to decide who's to represent us."

"What's it for?" Marge asked next.

"To 'vitalize social studies' he told the Juniors," Rod explained.

"Meaning what?" Marge asked.

"It probably means a rhubarb," Rod began. Then the bell sounded and Dr. Tozian stepped to the rostrum. Black hair, black eyes, tall and slender and young, he looked like an interesting teacher. But he didn't have a chance to greet his sophomore class. With a surprising clamour the inter-communication bell stopped him.

For a surprised second nobody moved. What could this announcement be? Even Dr. Tozian was not prepared for it.

"There will be a special all-school assembly on the east

lawn," they heard their superintendent announce. "All classes will follow the fire drill route out of the building at once."

It was Rod who spoke first, after the click-off sounded.

"Look, Dr. Tozian, if you don't know the fire drill route, I do," he said. "This room turns right and goes out the side door downstairs."

The social studies sophomores followed Dr. Tozian and Rod out of the building into the school yard where other classes equally surprised were assembling. At the far end of the school grounds a few tables and chairs from the lunchroom were lined up under the trees, and Superintendent Griffin was standing on a box with an old school bell in his hand. He waited until all of the classes were out before he rang it for attention.

"Boys and girls! You don't know how glad I am that all of you are out here on solid ground," he began. "Your high school building wasn't constructed to hold an enrollment such as we have this fall. When we took a pre-school registration last spring the figures did not approximate today's attendance. So I put through a telephone call to the State Education Department for I was fearful your combined weight would tax the structure beyond its capacity. I just got the facts a few minutes ago and I was right. You can't all be accommodated in the building at once. We're lucky the floors haven't caved in." He wiped his forehead and looked relieved.

Gasps and backward glances toward the old red brick building greeted the announcement. They had been in danger, and no one had suspected it except the superintendent.

"We shall have to operate school this year on a two-platoon system," Superintendent Griffin went on. "Have your parents decide whether they want you to attend in the morning from 7:30 to 11:30 or in the afternoon from 12:30 to 4.30. Tomorrow we'll re-arrange schedules. It's going to be hard on everyone but this is an emergency. The Board of Education is meeting in an extra session this afternoon and we'll have an announcement in *The Clarion* as soon as pos-

27

sible. Now we want you to spend the rest of the day organizing your extra-curricular activities and your clubs out here in the yard. I'll read off the names of the faculty advisors, then the senior boys can help Mr. Matthews bring out more chairs and tables and you can get started."

He read the list of the previous year's club advisors. Dr. Tozian was assigned the task of Debate Club coach, a responsibility his predecessor had carried. Without too much surprise, Marge saw Rod with the Debate crowd. He would sign up, of course, though Debate had not been one of his interests in the past.

Across the yard Janey signalled to her.

"We want to get the Journalism Club going right away," Janey explained. She had been elected editor just before school closed in the spring.

"This is big news. We must get a statement from Superintendent Griffin and get our first issue out Wednesday if we can, not next week. Find Rod and remind him he's business manager this year. He'll have to go down to *The Clarion* right away and see about getting the type set, and the deadlines for copy, and what an extra issue will cost."

Janey's eyes were shining with excitement and her enthusiasm was contagious.

"But it looks as though Rod is going out for Debate," Marge suggested.

"He can do both," Janey insisted. "He seemed eager to sign up for Journalism Club last spring and you signed up too, remember? You've got to read proof. This comes ahead of Debate or anything else, so hurry while I round up the class reporters!"

What else was there to do? This would have been the time to talk to Mr. Matthews about a Plastics Club. But now Bill Tanner was strolling across the grass toward Janey's table and Marge was afraid he would say something about Jerome. He might ask her where she had met him, and why he and Rod appeared to be such friends.

28

Where was Jerome now anyway, when the other students were gathering around the tables where clubs were organizing? She didn't see him anywhere, and she didn't want to talk to Bill about Jerome or Rod or anything or anybody.

"Okay," she told her sister quickly. "I'll go for Rod."

CHAPTER III

FLASH!

MARGE HURRIEDLY CROSSED the school yard to Dr. Tozian's table.

"I've got an assignment for you," she said. "Janey wants you to go down to *The Clarion* and find out what an additional issue of the school paper will cost. The Journalism Club wants to get out an extra Wednesday."

"What? Go now?" He sounded annoyed.

"She's rounding up the reporters and said we should get started," Marge told him. "This is big news." She knew she was echoing Janey, and the words didn't sound official when she said them. "You signed up for Journalism, remember?"

"Signed up? Got drafted, you mean!" He was frowning. "Janey thought I'd be the one for business manager because of Shorty . . . Shorty! Oh, no!"

Rod's thin jaw dropped and for a moment he stood and stared at her. Then his hands went into his pockets. "Have you got a dime?" he asked.

"I guess so. Why?"

"Come on! Will Shorty want to put me in chains! This is murder!"

"What do you mean?" Marge asked as he started to leave the school yard.

"Be ready to give with that dime," Rod said, hurrying toward the stationery store and pop stand where the boys and girls gathered after school. She wasn't sure they were supposed to leave the school yard, but Janey had told her to have Rod arrange for immediate publication of the extra. He must intend to do it by telephone. Inside the store he ducked into the phone booth.

Marge watched the tense motion of his cheeks and lips through the glass panel. She could tell that he had asked for Shorty but she couldn't hear anything he said, and when he opened the door to borrow her dime he closed it again tightly. It was plain that he was doing most of the talking. At last he came out.

"Well, can they set the type?" Marge asked. "What will it cost?"

"I don't know. We'll go down and see."

"You don't know? What on earth were you talking about?" she asked.

" 'This is big news,' remember?" he quoted her. "You were right, and dumb me not to think of it myself. There'd have been no living with Shorty if I hadn't called him. We'll go down to *The Clarion* now and see what we can negotiate. I'm afraid I've given away our bargaining power, but there may be such a thing as gratitude."

It was a minute before Marge realized what had been happening.

"You mean it'll be in the paper tonight? About our school, and the two platoons?"

"Everything I know," Rod admitted. "What I don't know Shorty can make up."

"Will Superintendent Griffin like that?" Marge asked. "He said there would be a piece in *The Clarion* later."

31

"There will be," Rod assured her. "Some stuffy statement by the Board of Education. Tonight there'll be news, in the 'Flash' column—a dozen lines probably, that Shorty's getting set right now. Come on."

"Maybe you'd better go without me," Marge hedged.

Rod sensed what was in her mind. "You didn't have any part in this," he assured her. "Janey told you to send me down, didn't she? She got us both to sign up for Journalism because we looked useful. Me because of Shorty and you because you can spell."

They were outside the store now and Marge looked across the street to the busy, noisy school yard, still hesitating. Fleetingly she thought of her father and his doubts about Rodney. She wouldn't be disobeying, and Janey had made the assignment.

"You've got to go down to the newspaper office every Tuesday after school to read proof, then you've got to check it again in the school print shop before the paper's run off there," Rod told her. "You might as well come along now and see the place, and find out if they'll set type for us right away."

Marge wanted to go. It sounded exciting, and besides the more she saw of Rodney the better she liked him. Some of his gruffness and cock-sureness were doubtless the result of living alone with his bachelor uncle.

Marge didn't know much about Rodney's life, but she did know Shorty had taken him several years ago when his mother became ill with tuberculosis. Both parents had gone to Arizona and his father had not returned to Eastfield after his mother died. Marge thought of it briefly while they walked the half mile to the newspaper office.

The Clarion building was one block off Main Street on the corner of a side street which once had been residential. It was the early home of Mr. Whiting's father. Above its new glass brick front the old walls of the original house, with gingerbread around the second story windows and the eaves, contrasted incongruously.

"We'll find Shorty in what he refers to as his office," Rod said, waving a greeting to a young lady behind a long counter, and pushing through a swinging half-door to a room beyond. "Shorty refuses to call it the 'city room.' He says any newspaper man from New York or Chicago would just laugh, but just the same it is the city room."

Marge had no idea of what a city room should look like. Here there were three long tables covered with papers. Two elderly women banged at typewriters, long galley proofs overflowed from wastepaper baskets, and one small bookcase was jammed with reference books, a dictionary, atlas and world almanac. Presiding over the confusion was a small man immaculate in a gray pin-stripe suit and gray necktie. Flies buzzed around the pastepot on Shorty's table, but propped safely against the wall were three handsome pieces of antique brass serving as ash tray, pencil holder and cigar box. On a carved walnut shelf above them an ornate French brass clock ticked rapidly.

Shorty was bent over a damp proof of the front page, his face tense, his thin hands closed so tightly that the knuckles were white. He glanced up when Marge and Rod stepped into the room and the expression on his face changed for an instant.

"Hello, Hi-Fi," he said. "Hello, Marge."

He didn't smile and he turned back to the page proof almost instantly, but his voice had welcomed them. "Want to see your story?" Once more his eyes sought Rodney's and it was plain that to Shorty this boy was not the "Hot Rod" the school had dubbed him.

Marge wondered how he knew who she was. She had seen him talking to Superintendent Griffin and looking in on high school athletic events, but she had never met him. Perhaps Rod had said they were coming. Anyway, he knew who she was and that both she and Rodney wanted to see the story about their school. They crowded close to read it, and she noticed Shorty gathering up some small pieces of paper and put-

33

ting them in his coat pocket instead of the wastebasket, before she became absorbed in the story.

"IT'S TWO PLATOONS

High School Building
Unsafe for Enrollment

"Eastfield High School held sessions in the school yard this afternoon and tonight their parents must decide between having teen-agers under foot all morning or all afternoon. When enrollment today totted up the largest figure on record, Superintendent Allen Griffin became alarmed. Would the old floors hold up under the load? A telephone call to the State Department of Education located the original building plans and confirmed his fears.

"This afternoon the Board of Education is meeting in extra session inside the century-old brick building while teachers and students try to do something constructive outside. An official statement from the Board to parents and taxpayers is expected in the next issue of *The Clarion*."

That was all. Just the few lines that Rod had correctly anticipated, set in bold type.

"Wonderful," Marge said when she finished reading. "Now we'll get a new school, with modern shops, maybe."

Shorty shook his head. "You'd be surprised how people hate to tax themselves," he cautioned. "Especially if they haven't any children of their own in school. You can't get a new school unless the property owners do vote to tax themselves."

"Most of the people here have children in school," Marge said. "You'd think they all did if you'd seen our classes today."

"But all of the people who have children in school aren't property owners and thus tax payers," Shorty explained. "Lesson one in economics. In our part of the world at least, only taxpayers can vote taxes. That's fair, isn't it?"

His scant eyebrows were up and he looked at her questioningly. "It will be interesting to see whether you get a new school or a pre-fab annex."

"Right now I'll settle for type to print an extra issue of the school paper for the school we've got," Rod interrupted. "Do we get it tomorrow? And for free, since we gave you a scoop?"

"Tomorrow, yes. For free, no." Shorty clipped off the answers. "For cost, maybe. Why don't you show Marge the pressroom while I check these outrageous demands with the Chief. Blackmail, I call them." He winked at Marge and disappeared through a door which Marge guessed might lead to the office of the owner. Recalling Mr. Whiting, Marge was sure the type would not be free.

Marge didn't think much of the composing room which Rod took her through first. One of the three linotype machines clicked in a metallic monotone, there were galleys of inked type on a long, stone-topped bench, some high cases with narrow drawers which she guessed might hold hand type, and everything was dark and dirty and oily looking. She wondered where she would sit when she came down each Tuesday to read the galley proofs. Not here, she hoped. Two or three men, arms and hands stained black with printer's ink, stopped their work to stare at her and she felt uncomfortable.

Rod tried to explain how the big press worked while he led her through the pressroom. The only thing that was clear to Marge when the dark monster began to roar, was the surprising manner in which the individual papers were folded and cut, after the paper had wound its way from an immense roll of newsprint through the intricate black rollers of the machine. She was glad when Rod motioned to an open door leading into the alley. There, grabbing the papers from a moving canvas belt, was Jerry. Shirt open at the neck, sleeves rolled above his elbows, he was counting out the proper number of papers for the little group of waiting newsboys, and he didn't see her.

"Why don't you wait here and walk back with us when Jerry finishes my job?" Rod asked. "I'll join you after I see what sort of deal Shorty works out with the boss."

With his one free hand he pushed her down onto an old packing box, tapped Jerry on the shoulder, then went back into the newspaper office.

Marge framed the words, "May I wait?" with her lips and

tried to smile. She wasn't sure she wanted to walk along the business street and up to the school yard with Jerry. She wasn't sure he would welcome her, either. But after a moment's hesitation he grinned, then pushed at the touseled head of one of the waiting newsboys who giggled at the sight of Marge.

When Rod returned he was triumphant. "We get the extra for cost," he announced. "I thought Shorty would come through. And here's your dime, Marge. Thanks."

Together they walked up Main Street, Rod showing Jerry where to leave the papers.

"Maybe we can still see Mr. Matthews," Marge suggested as they walked along. "He couldn't hold any classes this afternoon, but he'll probably stay until the Clubs are all organized and the tables and chairs back in the lunchroom."

"Have you thought of what this two platoon system means to the teachers?" Rod asked. "They won't get through with classes until 4:30 and they'll have to start at 7:30 in the morning. From the rumbling this afternoon, I wonder if we're going to have any Clubs."

"Not any Clubs?" Marge repeated.

"This new Dr. Tozian came right out and said if he coached Debate it would have to be for half an hour at noon," Rod reported. "He's got a full class schedule and responsibilities at home. When he balked openly, the rest of them backed him and refused to say they'd do it. Just shut up like a dead radio on the subject. Didn't you see?"

Marge had been too busy to notice. "Even Mr. Matthews?" she asked forlornly.

"Eight hours in school is eight hours, to say nothing of papers to correct for twice as many kids as last year," Rod reminded her. "Maybe we'll get less homework. Now there's a thought!"

"What about Jerry's woodworking course?" Marge asked. "What about driver education? This is my year for that."

"Mr. Matthews will take me in advanced woodworking," Jerry said, speaking for the first time. "You should have seen the enrollment there this morning! Not a bad shop he's got, down next to the boiler room! But do you need a new school!"

"They'll go on with driver education, Marge," Rod assured her. "That was a regular part of the school program. They won't drop any courses we had last year."

Abruptly Rod stopped and pointed to a store across the street which had been empty for months. In front, a big green truck was parked. It carried the name of an Andover City radio firm in black and gold letters across the side.

"This is Jerry's headquarters," Rod explained to Marge. Then, to Jerry, "You shouldn't have any trouble signing up this new customer. Mind if I have a look-see?"

Without waiting for a reply, he darted across the street. For a moment Marge hesitated and Jerry looked at her doubtfully.

"Okay, so come on," Jerry finally said and they followed Rod who was talking to a broad-shouldered man in dark blue trousers and a frayed white shirt. Rod introduced him as Mr. Chamberlin, and he smiled at Marge in a friendly, inquiring way.

"Mr. Chamberlin's opening a radio-television-record shop here in Eastfield. Hard to believe, isn't it?" Rod said. "Repairs and everything."

"I've worked for the Andover City firm for fifteen years," Mr. Chamberlin explained. "When I said I'd like a shop of my own, they backed me. Now you kids won't have to waste money on gasoline and burn up the road to Andover City when you want the latest albums." He laughed nervously when he said it and avoided looking at his son.

"If you need a helper—more than Jerry, I mean—I'm your boy," Rod said. "I'll spend all you pay me right here, assembling a Hi-Fi set. That's for me!"

Hi-Fi, Marge thought. Shorty was the one who really knew Rod.

"I'd figured on Jerry helping after school," Mr. Chamberlin admitted, with a hasty glance at his son. "I don't know. I'll have to find out about hours a minor is allowed to work. We never hired kids in Andover City and I don't know." Again he hesitated and watched the young people speculatively. "Drop by after I get things set up, why don't you?"

"I sure will," Rod said. "This arm will be out of a sling before too long. With school on a two-platoon system I'll have more time than ever . . . unless Jerry . . ." He left the sentence unfinished and glanced at Jerry questioningly.

"What's on your mind?" Jerry asked.

"Maybe you'd like to keep this newspaper job," Rod suggested. "Maybe we could exchange jobs. Shorty's had me counting out papers ever since I was born, it seems like."

Jerry shrugged. "I suppose we've got to do something with ourselves," he said still avoiding his father's eyes. "We can see."

"It looks as though everybody's going to do something they like except me," Marge observed.

"It looks as though your father and Janey are out scouting for you now," Rod told her, gesturing toward the old station wagon coming down the hill. Dad was driving, Janey in the front seat beside him. They came to a halt at the curb.

"Did you get everything set?" Janey called before Marge and the boys reached the car. "I thought you'd never come back, so when Dad drove by I hailed him. Oh, Dad, you haven't met Rodney Maguire or Jerome Chamberlin. Jerry's a newcomer here."

"No, I haven't met them. Hello, Rodney . . . Jerome." Dad sounded casual but Marge knew nothing was escaping him. She turned from the station wagon to watch the few people passing Main Street's stores,—the gift shop, the two grocery stores, all so familiar that she didn't really see them.

Was Rodney going to measure up, arm in a sling, bluejeans plaster-tight on his thin legs, T-shirt open at the neck? How could she expect Dad to see him as Shorty saw him, as she did? Would Dad relent and say she might go out with Rodney if he ever asked her?

Perhaps Rodney sensed the quiet scrutiny. He acknowledged the introduction then gave Janey the information she wanted almost gruffly.

"Get your copy down to Shorty by noon tomorrow and the type will be ready for Marge to proofread after school," he said. "Shorty managed the deal for us at cost."

"Wonderful!" Janey beamed. "Everybody in Journalism Club is working tonight. Now does anybody want a ride anywhere? Dad's on his way to the station to meet some of the trustees. Anyone going that way?"

Rod shook his head. "I'm having to teach Jerry my route," he explained.

Jerry, who hadn't said a word during the brief exchange, turned to Rod.

"What about the gift shop?" he asked, ignoring Janey and her father.

"Customer," Rod told him.

Jerry's arm rose easily and the folded paper hurtled through the air—into the face of the proprietoress who stepped out of her door at that exact moment. She reeled, glasses flying, and caught at the door to keep from falling.

For a terrifying second everybody seemed paralyzed. Then Dad jumped from the car and Mr. Chamberlin rushed from his shop, reaching her first and retrieving her glasses.

The woman, whom Marge remembered as Mrs. Clarke, pushed her graying hair out of her face.

"Rodney didn't mean to do it," she gasped.

"It wasn't Rodney," Mr. Chamberlin said quickly. "It was my boy. Rodney has a broken wrist. I'll pay for the glasses. Are you sure you're all right?"

Marge heard Jerome muttering under his breath. "My old man to the rescue again! Why did she have to come out at that split second?"

Startled, both Marge and Janey stared at the boys. Weren't either of them even going to apologize to Mrs. Clarke?

As though sensing her thoughts, Jerry spoke again. "She's all right. Let's move on, Rod."

39

"We can't," Rod said and started toward the store. Marge breathed easier. Rod at least was making a decent gesture. Jerry walked away from the car.

"I hate this town," he mumbled loudly enough for Marge and Janey to hear.

Satisfied that Mrs. Clarke was not hurt, Dad returned to the car. In silence he started the motor, waved briefly to Rod who was still standing with Mrs. Clarke and Mr. Chamberlin, and started slowly down Main Street, his two daughters beside him.

It was Janey who spoke finally. "I didn't know you were going to the newspaper office," she said, overlooking the unfortunate incident. "It's all right, only what kept you so long?"

"It didn't seem so long," Marge replied. "We read the story about our school in the page proof, then Rod took me through the plant and I waited to walk back with the boys, and . . ."

"The story about our school?" Janey gasped. "Superintendent Griffin said it would be in the paper after the Board decides what to do."

Marge wished she hadn't mentioned the story. They would have seen it in another hour; time enough to question her then.

"Marge, how did the story get in the paper so fast?" her father asked. "Did you and Rodney go down there and tell Rodney's uncle?"

"No. At least I didn't," Marge answered. "Rod told me to come along because tomorrow after school I have to go down and proofread."

"Did Rodney give the story to *The Clarion?*" her father pressed.

"Rod telephoned it in," Marge admitted. She knew Rod would not have denied it.

"You're sure you didn't tell Mr. Maguire any of it?" He sounded very insistent.

"I didn't talk to him about it at all," Marge said. "It was all in the paper when we got there. It's only two or three short paragraphs. They set the type while we walked down from school."

Her father sighed with relief. "I don't see why *The Clarion* couldn't have waited until the Board decided what to do and say," he observed.

"Well, you can't really blame the paper, Dad," Janey reasoned. "News is news when it happens. I'm breaking my neck to get out an extra. I just hope *The Clarion* got it right."

Marge started to say the story was correct. She wanted to ask her father if he blamed Rodney for telling his uncle, but as she started to speak she saw her father's jaw set. He was looking straight ahead, tense and unsmiling. She turned her eyes to the passing street scene and said nothing.

CHAPTER IV

EASTFIELD GETS AN OFFER

Marge had come to expect that visitors at the Ragland home would be important people. Deans and presidents of other colleges, members of Dr. Ragland's Board of Trustees, senators and representatives and even the governor now and then, were the Raglands' guests. It was on those occasions that Mother's rare values were most evident. She had done the reading Dad hadn't had time for. She set a beautiful table with double damask linen, rare old china and silver candle sticks. The Brundage's maid always found someone who could come in to serve and wash dishes.

This dinner was just like the others, except that before it was over Marge realized Janey was very quiet. She didn't finish the food on her plate and scarcely touched her dessert. When Mother led the way to the living room Janey stayed behind and Marge saw her talking seriously with Dad for a few minutes, then she disappeared upstairs.

Marge waited in the hall, wondering whether the guests would go to Dad's study, leaving the living room television to her, or whether she must find some other diversion. There had been no homework assignments. Finally she followed Janey upstairs to their room where the typewriter had begun to click rapidly.

"What are you writing?" Marge asked.

"I had an idea during dinner and Dad said it might be good," Janey explained. "I've got to check it with Superintendent Griffin in the morning."

"What is it?"

"I don't think I'll tell even you," Janey replied. "I think it's so terrific I'll die if Superintendent Griffin doesn't want me to use it."

Long ago Marge had learned she could not change Janey's mind. She surveyed their room, still wondering what to do. It had been a dainty, blue and white room until last year when Janey began to think seriously of college. Then the flowered wall paper had been replaced by a subdued green with brown and gold stripes, the dainty counterpanes gave way to brown corduroy, and the bookcases merged their unobtrusive olive green shelves into the wall. It looked like the picture of a college girl's study-bedroom which Janey had found in one of her mother's magazines. Marge had agreed reluctantly to the change; it wasn't the homey room that had been theirs ever since she could remember.

She looked questioningly at Janey. The typing had stopped and her sister was staring in her direction and biting her lip thoughtfully.

"Are you going to attend school mornings or afternoons?" Marge asked.

"That's what I was thinking about," Janey said. "It might be a good idea if we split it and I take the afternoon shift at school. Then if I ever get stuck and have to work on copy all morning, I could meet you at noon and you could race down to *The Clarion* right after lunch. Tomorrow, for instance. It may be noon before I can get this checked with Superintendent Griffin."

"Sounds reasonable," Marge agreed. "I have to be at the newspaper office one afternoon at least on the weeks the school paper comes out to read proof. It would be better if I got school out of the way in the mornings."

Janey resumed her typing and Marge picked up a book she hadn't finished, but her mind was on Janey's idea, now being banged out only a few feet away. Finally she put the book aside.

"I guess I'll go call Carol and see when she's going to school," she told her sister and went to the extension telephone in the hall. She stretched out on the floor.

Her friend was full of news.

"I've been calling all the kids," Carol told her. "Alphabetically, and I was almost down to you. I wanted to be sure somebody I like goes to school in the afternoons when I've got to go. We drew lots and Lois got the morning shift. When are you going?"

"Mornings, if it's all right with Mother," Marge replied. "We're splitting it."

"Lucky you!" Carol exclaimed. "All the boys who go out for athletics will be in school mornings, so they'll have afternoons to practice. That means I'll never see Lewis Tanner. But you're all right. Rod's going mornings too, so he can work in Mr. Chamberlin's shop afternoons. If he can get the job, and if Jerome will continue with the newspaper route. All the boys will be in school mornings and all the girls in the afternoons, practically." It was a wail.

"Does Rod really think he can get a job in the new radio store?" Marge asked.

"Well, he practically has a job there," Carol said, repeating her favorite and over-worked adverb. "You know how standoffish Jerry was when people tried to be friendly. I found out why. He didn't want to move to Eastfield. He doesn't want to play against his old school, even though he didn't make the Andover team. And he doesn't get along with his Dad. Don't ask me why. So Rod thinks maybe . . ."

44

"Did Rod tell you all this?" Marge asked, wondering when. "How did he find out?"

"He said after they finished the newspaper route Jerry said he was going to hitchhike to Andover, so Rod went back and helped Mr. Chamberlin in the store the rest of the afternoon. Dusted off the albums and things like that. So he found out."

Marge thought she knew what Rod would do with the money he earned if he got the job but she didn't tell Carol. If Rod had felt frustrated because there was no electronics course at school he had kept it to himself and settled for woodworking. She'd not talk.

She saw Rodney the next morning when she reported for school. He was with a group of boys and girls at the bulletin board where Mr. Matthews was posting a notice. Marge joined them. A large poster was already up and the headline read:

INDUSTRY OFFERS SCHOOLS AN INDUSTRIAL ARTS AWARDS PROGRAM

"What's this, Mr. Matthews?" Rod and Bill asked at the same time.

"Is it for girls too?" Marge chimed in.

"What are the awards?" Bill asked, reading the notice. "Trophies? Money?"

Mr. Matthews pointed to the poster. "There are cash prizes for a lot of things. Even your plastics, Marge. The trouble is, all entries have to be class work, done in school shops, so all we can enter is the wood classification. If we'd managed to get a plastics course included, you could have entered, Marge. One of our new boys, Jerome, has a chance, though. There are cash awards offered at the Regional Student Craftsmen's Fairs that precede the international judging at Greenfield Village in Dearborn, and national scholarships."

"Scholarships?" Bill asked, more interested now. "What colleges?"

"Not a scholarship for woodworking?" Rod sounded incredulous.

"I don't think so much of this," Bill announced when he had finished reading. "If you're going to college, Rod, why don't you take law or science? There's a real need for scientists today. The boys have jobs before they finish their courses."

Bill stood beside the bulletin board, books in hand, as serious as though the question of what Rod took was the national high school debate topic of the year.

"I wasn't thinking of the scholarship for myself," Rod said. "I was thinking of Jerry. Could he make a breakfront, Mr. Matthews? You know what happened."

Mr. Matthews nodded. "He's already talked to me about making one," he said. "But he'll have to select a simpler design than the one he wants to make. We'd need a shaper for that model, and our school shop doesn't have a shaper. They cost money!"

"Simplicity in design and line is supposed to be good," Marge chimed in, remembering some of Janey's arguments for changing their room at home. "I wish girls could try out for some of these prizes. We could if we had the right school shops."

"School shops!" Bill sounded scornful. "All I seem to hear is 'school shops.' I know they're okay, Mr. Matthews, but if we get a new school I hope you'll put the shops as far away from the study halls as possible. When a person's trying to concentrate and in the next room it's Bang! Bang! Bang! . . ."

Bill was always studying. He was going to be a lawyer like his father, Eastfield's only attorney. He hammered on the wall for emphasis with his books, and Marge jumped back as the bulletin board came down in a cloud of dust and plaster crumbs. The group of students scattered.

"Oh, no! Now I've done it," Bill immediately apologized "This school is really falling to pieces. I didn't mean to knock the bulletin board down, Mr. Matthews."

"Well, now that you have, do you know how to put it back up?" Mr. Matthews asked.

"Why, yes," Bill said, but he didn't sound too sure of himself. "A bigger nail. . . ."

Mr. Matthews turned away without replying.

"Go get a brace and drill," he said to Rod. "Be sure the shank fits the brace."

"About a ⅜ inch drill?" Rod asked, surveying the holes in the wall.

"And a couple of pieces of pine for the plugs," Mr. Matthews added, then turned to Bill. "If you want to know 'Why Industrial Arts,' stay around."

Bill hesitated. "I wouldn't be any help. I know I'm no good at this sort of thing," he said. "I'm sorry I knocked it down." He started for the stairs.

Marge watched him go with a feeling of satisfaction. This time he hadn't known all the answers. It was Rod and Mr. Matthews who knew what to do in an emergency.

"Do you think Jerry could win the scholarship?" she asked after both boys were gone.

"He has the best chance of anyone at Eastfield," Mr. Matthews said. "He's had two years at Andover City and I've seen their shops and the work the boys exhibited at their last open house. It might mean a great deal to Eastfield if he did win. I'm sure we can work out a design that will have a chance."

Marge picked up the Industrial Arts Awards notice that had fallen from the board. Jerry could make a real success of this, she was thinking. Only where was he this morning, if all the boys were going to school mornings, as Carol had said. Where had he gone after he left Rod yesterday afternoon? And the accident with the newspaper. It hadn't been Jerry's fault. He hadn't intended to hit Mrs. Clarke, but why hadn't he at least said he was sorry? She hoped no one knew about that except herself and Janey and Rod.

"Winning a scholarship would make people see that we do need more school shops, wouldn't it, Mr. Matthews?" Marge asked. "Everyone can't be a scholar and a genius. Look at these classifications! Ceramics, copper, aluminum, jewelry design. . . ."

Mr. Matthews surveyed the wall instead, while Marge studied the pictures of winners in other years. They made her wonder if Jerry could really compete. Mr. Matthews—comfortable, stocky, steady Mr. Matthews had said he might, and Mr. Matthews was a man people could trust.

Marge began daydreaming again while she walked to *The Clarion*. She looked in every store window, studying the display fixtures. Many were made of clear Plexiglas or lucite. In the gift shop window there was a display of key ring charms, pill boxes, and desk sets, beautifully carved and colored. Maybe there could be a Plastics Club after all, if she tried harder to get Mr. Matthews to organize one. She would talk to Rod about it if he was at the newspaper office tonight after she had read the proofs. The proofs! She hadn't thought of Janey's surprise article since last night. Janey had taken the copy to the newspaper office herself that forenoon.

Marge quickened her steps and almost dashed past the girl at the long counter in the newspaper office, and through the swinging door. Shorty was at his long table and she discovered immediately that the galleys he was looking at were the ones she had come to read.

"Great idea Janey has come up with," Shorty greeted her, scarcely glancing up from the proofs. She wasn't sure whether he approved until he handed the long sheets of paper to her. His thin face was expressionless as usual but his eyes were shining.

"This is quite a day for news," he told her. "Sit here at my table and I'll show you the proofreading marks. You put 'em in the margin whenever you find an error."

He spoke in the short-clipped sentences she remembered while he cleared a place.

"Page One Editorial, H. S. Job," the galley was marked.

Then, in the largest type the school paper ever used, she read the headline:

PARENTS! RIGHT THIS WAY, PLEASE

Eastfield High School Needs You Now

Marge read the two lines and looked at Shorty questioningly.

"So you didn't know," he observed with satisfaction.

Marge shook her head. "Janey cleared it with Superintendent Griffin," she said.

"I didn't doubt that," Shorty said. "I just wondered if she kept her scoop to herself."

"She sure did!" Marge commented and turned back to the story.

> "For the first time in the history of Eastfield, its high school this week went on a two platoon system. Students will attend school only half a day, but teachers will work from 7:30 in the morning to 4:30 in the afternoon. Classrooms will not be available for club programs until the hour when extracurricular activities were ending last year. But half of the student body will have been idle half a day, and teachers will be too tired to work any longer.

> "*Eastfield High School News* believes there are places in town where we could meet. What churches and lodges will give us meeting places? The Parent Teacher Association has already volunteered to help find club leaders. The school paper will act as a clearing house to schedule hours, places and leaders. Here are the clubs we operated last year which now need your help."

The list followed. It didn't contain any new clubs, of course. Marge felt breathless when she finished reading. Janey's own ardor carried through in the sincerity of her appeal.

"Your sister got her paper off to a good start," Marge heard Shorty saying. "I can think of people who could lead every one of those clubs. Dramatics, glee club, debate. I'll pick up Janey's idea in my next column and give you kids a boost."

"That would do it," Marge said gratefully. "It seems as

49

75641

though it would do more than save the activities program."
She was remembering what Shorty had said about taxpayers
who might not vote for a new school. In some way it might
influence them, only it wasn't clear enough in her mind for
her to mention it.

When she had finished reading the proofs and stacked them
together, she sat for a few minutes at Shorty's table, fingering
the shining brass ash tray in front of her and listening to the
typewriters clicking behind her. If only she had an idea half
as good to help get some industrial arts shops!

"Finished?" Shorty's question brought her back to reality.

"Yes. I hope I found all of the mistakes." She pushed the
proofs toward him and he began reading, running a long fore-
finger rapidly beneath each line. He found only one mistake
she had missed.

"Are you going to wait until *The Clarion* is out and walk
back with Jerry?" he asked, stacking the sheets together.
"Rod'll be along by the time the press starts rolling, I imagine. He's probably hanging around Chamberlin's, hoping
for a job."

She hurried through the pressroom to the alley where the
newsboys waited. Behind her the press was grinding and
groaning noisily and Marge could see the pressman starting
and stopping it, turning a handle here and adjusting something else there, until at last it operated smoothly. Then, as
the steady roar began and papers started moving down the
wide belt, Marge started for her little box seat in the alley.

Jerome was not there! Neither was Rod! And the papers
were beginning to tumble off the wide belt and pile up on the
ground in a scrambled heap.

Marge looked at the bewildered newsboys. "Go get Shorty,"
she shouted to the largest one. "Go on! Don't just stand there!
Hurry!"

The boy hesitated a moment, then raced to the front of
the building. It seemed hours as Marge struggled to grab the
papers and pile them on the ground, before Shorty got there.

One look and he tossed his coat onto Marge's box. His hands moved faster than the conveyor belt and he began counting out for the boys, disregarding the piles Marge had stacked on the ground. From the set of his lean jaws, Marge knew he was furious. Why had both boys ignored this responsibility? She felt herself trembling while she watched the reporter take over.

"Next! How many?" he shouted to the boys. One by one they stepped forward and gave him their count, filled their carrying bags, and with sly glances at each other and at Shorty, left to deliver their papers.

Neither Rod nor Jerry had appeared when at last the black giant slowed to a stop. Without a word Shorty motioned to one of the men inside the building, pointed to the mound of papers at his feet.

"Let's straighten 'em up and get 'em inside," he said.

"Mr. Whiting'll have apoplexy if his papers are late getting out," the man observed, stacking the loose papers together. "What happened to Rod?"

Marge didn't hear Shorty's answer. Mechanically she reached for one of the papers. She would see what the School Board had to say, what Shorty had written in his column, and then she would have to go home, whether Rod or Jerome had come or not.

Inch-high type, across all eight columns, demanded attention and she turned the paper right side up, expecting the statement by the Board. Instead the headline screamed:

INDUSTRY OFFERS TO BUY
DODD PARK

"What!" Marge exclaimed aloud, although there was no one to hear her.

The main facts of the story were in the first paragraph. Friday night the town aldermen would consider selling the waste land along the river. The mayor had received the offer earlier in the week. If the sale was approved five hundred new families would be added to Eastfield a year after the development was completed, and more as the industry expanded.

Five hundred more families for Eastfield! If there were four people to a family, Eastfield would soon rival Andover City in size.

Marge had read only the first two paragraphs when she sensed that Shorty had come back and was watching her.

"Well, what do you think?" he asked.

"Without really thinking, I'd say the aldermen should vote to sell," she said. "It's nothing but waste land that's flooded almost every spring. Only how could they build a factory there? It would be knee-deep in water once a year."

"You haven't read the whole story," Shorty told her, trying to sound casual. "They propose to build a dam and make an artificial lake. We'll have the architect's drawing in the next issue, before the aldermen meet."

His eyes were on the street beyond the alley, but he went on talking in even tones.

"The drawing will give people something to think about. Maybe make some of the aldermen hesitate before they turn it down. Big brick factory and a parking lot full of cars. New houses below where we live . . . a new real estate development. . . ."

"There wouldn't be any question of a new school if there were 500 more families, would there?" Marge asked. "We'd have to get one. Maybe a school like the one we kids want."

"There'd have to be more than a high school," Shorty told her. "A couple of elementary schools too, and a lot of other changes. That's the rub."

Marge wondered what he meant and looked at him inquiringly.

"Can't you figure it?" he asked.

"I suppose Alexander Dodd's not going to want another bank in town," she suggested. "And the Brundages have all the automobile business as it is." The image of Mrs. Brundage, tall, thin, commanding, her short, faded blond hair dishevelled by every breeze, might not make the newcomers so servile.

"You're not so slow," Shorty said. "The merchants would like to see it happen. They're the aldermen and they cast the vote, but one way or another . . ." He hesitated as though he had already said too much.

"I'll bet my father will favor it," Marge said. "He's working now to get more dormitories and buildings for the college, because it's growing."

Shorty said h-m-m-m-m. "As it is now, the college has the biggest payroll in town. It wouldn't have, if this sale went through. Would the faculty like to see men with dinner pails walking along our peaceful, half-asleep streets?"

"But the college is way up on the hill," Marge reminded him. "The students almost never come to Dodd Park, even to play ball. They have their own athletic field."

"I could be wrong," Shorty admitted. He was tapping his foot nervously now.

Marge got up from her little box, feeling worse than ever. Shorty could be right, too. Perhaps her father would oppose the new industry, which seemed to assure her of what she wanted when a new school was built.

And where, oh where were Rod and Jerry? Why hadn't they been here to take care of the newsboys today when the biggest story in the history of Eastfield had broken?

CHAPTER V

SHATTERED GLASS

MARGE WALKED HOME as slowly as she could, pretending to read one of her school books but actually thinking of her father. It was fortunate that Shorty had warned her he might not favor selling Dodd Park. Otherwise she probably would have dashed into the house eager to tell of Shorty's scoop. Now she would wait until she knew what her father thought before she said anything.

Janey and Bill were on the side porch talking excitedly when she got home and Dad was holding the paper on his knees, looking thoughtfully into the soft green of the forsythia bushes. The newsboy had reached Jewett Avenue ahead of her.

"I hope the aldermen will vote that down in a hurry," Bill said as she came up the brick steps. "Five hundred families, all with kids like this Jerome Chamberlin, probably."

Marge wondered if he were putting Rod in the same category, for he avoided looking at her and had scarcely said "hello" when she came onto the porch.

"It's hard to think of Eastfield as being different than it is," Janey seemed to agree. "Imagine coming home from college and finding the town another Andover City!"

"You can't expect Eastfield to stay the same, Janey," her father said. "I'm working to get new dormitories so we can house more students at the college next year."

"That's different," Bill protested. "Enlarging the campus, and workers' shacks along the river are two different things."

Dad ran a hand over his short, thin hair. "Workers don't live in shacks any more," he corrected Bill. "Skilled craftsmen earn more than my faculty members. An efficient, profit-making industry could more or less control our political life, and influence our cultural and social life. There is a great deal to be considered, and carefully, before Dodd Park is sold."

Marge dropped her school books on the porch table and sat down. Dad's cautious words seemed to confirm Shorty's surmise that he might not approve the sale.

"I'm sure you're right, sir," Bill agreed. "A change in population would make a great difference here. I personally hope it never happens."

"You don't even want us to have modern shops in our new school, do you?" Marge asked. Bill might as well come out for or against an up-to-date school, too. He would be gone in another year and his younger brother Lewis was just a junior edition of Bill, she had always thought. She realized they were all looking at her now, and she hoped her summer tan would hide the flush she felt in her cheeks and neck. It was the first time she had ever indicated how she felt about Bill.

He didn't answer her directly. "We haven't got a new school yet," he said with a forced laugh, getting up and moving toward the steps. "That appeal by the School Board doesn't sound as though they were certain of overwhelming support. Well, good night, Dr. Ragland. Janey. I'll be seeing you."

He extended a hand in the direction of Marge's short locks, but she pulled away.

"Marge, I think you were rude to Bill," Janey said as soon as he was out of hearing. "What made you say that?" At almost the same time Dad asked another question.

"When did you become so interested in school shops?"

"I read a story about a girl who's paying her way through college by making things of plastics," Marge told her father, disregarding Janey. "After she finishes, she's going to have a manufacturing business of her own. It's something different a girl could do. Then the Industrial Arts Awards notice came along. We could enter that if Mr. Matthews had the right equipment for advanced courses. He doesn't have what he needs so Jerry can make the breakfront he wants. He may have a chance at the scholarship though," she added. That should please Janey.

"What is this Industrial Arts Awards?" Dad turned to Janey when he asked the question, and she, not Marge, explained. She was going to have a write-up about it in the next issue of her school newspaper.

"I didn't know Jerome wanted to try out for the scholarship," Janey admitted when she finished. "How did you find that out, Marge?"

"I was there when Mr. Matthews posted the notice and they were talking about it," Marge said quickly. "You can ask Bill. He was there too."

"Are you girls on the verge of a quarrel?" Dad asked, reaching for his brief case. "You weren't very pleasant to Bill, Marge."

Marge had thought Dad understood her feeling about Bill, but again, as on the night of the accident, she hesitated to say openly that she didn't like him.

More important, however, was Dad's stand on selling Dodd Park, and Marge didn't want the conversation to end without being sure of what he thought.

"I didn't mean to be rude, but he seems to be against everything new," she said. "Do you think the aldermen should turn down the sale, Dad?"

56

He got up and started inside. "I couldn't say 'yes' or 'no' without finding out all about the industry that wants to buy," he said. "This article doesn't give us enough information. The aldermen should investigate that thoroughly."

It wasn't the answer Marge had hoped for. She wanted to come out openly in favor of the sale when she saw her friends in school the next day, but now she couldn't. She wondered what Janey was going to say, but Janey gathered up her books and followed her father inside, leaving Marge alone on the porch. With regret Marge saw her sister disappear. She hadn't intended to quarrel with her. She had meant to tell Janey her first editorial was wonderful, and to let her know Shorty was going to support it in his column, but Bill had driven the editorial out of her mind.

Marge tried to talk to Janey that evening when they went upstairs to study.

"What are you going to say about Dodd Park tomorrow?" Marge asked.

"I think Dad told us plainly enough what we should say," Janey replied coolly.

"If you're angry with me about Bill, I'm sorry. Only Bill isn't always so considerate of other people," Marge defended herself. "I think he's opinionated."

"At least he has intelligent opinions," Janey answered her. "I'm nice to your friends and I think you should be nice to mine. I'd even be nice to Rodney if you ever invited him home, and I don't approve of him altogether!"

There was no mistaking that. Janey opened her books with an air of finality.

The next day at school everyone was talking about Dodd Park. Marge watched for a glimpse of Rod, or even Jerome. It was not until social studies that she saw Rodney and he avoided her eyes.

Dr. Tozian made no effort to stop the excited conversation. When the bell rang he clapped his hands together, then plunged into a more orderly discussion.

57

"If Eastfield had a Chamber of Commerce, this issue would get first consideration," he said. "We'll organize our Chamber of Commerce right away, and this will be one of the first things we'll study. Who wants to suggest another important civic issue?"

Marge's hand went up at once. "Our new school," she said. "I think the kids are the ones most concerned and we should have something to say about the school we want. We could even have a campaign of some sort to let the taxpayers know."

"I'd hoped someone would suggest that," Dr. Tozian said with a smile. "I notice you said the taxpayers. Why?"

Marge was glad Shorty had explained it to her and she could give a clear reply.

"It's all tied up now with the Dodd Park sale," Rod broke in when she had finished. "If enough new families moved in, and bought homes, they could vote. A lot of little voters can out-vote a few big property owners. And people working for industry would be more likely to want a school with modern vocational courses."

Marge was sure Rod had gotten his information from Shorty too. The whole class was looking at them and she felt a thrill of elation.

"We want something beside academic courses, and now before we're through high school," Marge declared.

Dr. Tozian's dark eyes glanced from student to student, encouraging them to talk.

"In Armenia, where my people came from, they have a saying that everyone should have a silver bracelet," he told them. "And what do you think that silver bracelet is? It is a manual skill. Something a person can fall back upon, no matter how he may rise in the world, or how adversity may strike." Again he looked around the room. "I can see where some of you agree with that. And I can see where the sophomores have some good candidates for the Chamber of Commerce."

"If we can start organizing, I'd like to nominate Marge," Rod announced.

The murmur of approval was a complete surprise to Marge.

She hadn't been selected for any office or position of leadership during her freshman year, but her classmates were ready to vote for her now. Before the session ended they had selected Marge and Rod as their representatives. Dr. Tozian announced that the new organization would be completed at once, with two members from each of the two class groups, or a total of sixteen in all. They would attend the meeting of the aldermen Friday night to learn how local government was carried on when an important issue was at stake.

It happened so fast Marge could scarcely believe it. She wondered, when it was over, whether she should have accepted the office. If Shorty hadn't told her how schools were voted into existence, she would have sat quietly and let others do the talking. Would she be able to carry on as the class expected?

It worried her, but she could hardly wait to tell Mother and Janey and Dad. This feeling of leadership was new and exciting. Janey had always known it. Now Marge and Janey would have something in common; something to share as equals. Dad could be proud of her, too.

Marge told her mother of her unexpected recognition as soon as she got home. Mother put her arms around Marge and held her close.

"We'll keep it a secret until dinner time and then you can tell," she said. "I'm sure you'll do well."

"There's one thing that bothers me, though," Marge confessed. "I wouldn't have been chosen if Shorty hadn't told me things the other kids didn't know. Maybe Rod wouldn't, either." She looked to her mother for reassurance.

"Rod will always have Shorty to turn to, and you'll have Dad," Mother said. "If there's any doubt in your mind, try to avoid positive statements until you've had an opportunity to check with your father. You can always 'hedge for time' as they say."

Marge's announcement at the dinner table came as a real surprise to both Janey and Dad.

"You and Rod!" Janey exclaimed. "That *is* an honor. The

Chamber of Commerce is going to be the most exciting thing in school this year."

"You know about it, then?" Dad asked Janey. "Are you a member?"

"No, and I was disappointed too," Janey admitted. "I guess the seniors thought Journalism and Drama and Language Clubs were enough for one person. They did elect Bill, of course." She pronounced his name with considerable satisfaction.

"Are you going to take up important local issues?" her father questioned. "And go to the meeting of the town aldermen?" He wasn't exactly frowning, but he looked serious.

"Yes," Marge answered quickly before Janey could speak for her again. "We're to meet Dr. Tozian at the high school entrance and go to town hall together."

"H-m-m-m-m. You're sure you understood correctly?"

"I'm sure," Marge insisted. "That's what Dr. Tozian said."

"I think she's right," Janey agreed. "Dr. Tozian said the same thing to the seniors."

"If you girls don't mind, I'll call Superintendent Griffin," Dad said when he had finished his apple cobbler. "I'd just like to be sure."

He didn't close the study door or attempt to keep his questions from them. He wanted to know if the girls had understood, he said. "After all, Marge is pretty young." Then he kept saying "H-m-m-m-m" and "I see," and finally said it must be all right if Superintendent Griffin had such confidence in Dr. Tozian.

Marge felt both relieved and let down. All the honors that had come to Janey had been greeted at home as achievements. Her election to the Chamber of Commerce was a source for concern. It probably wasn't an achievement, she admitted to herself. It was a fluke and she well might regret it. She began worrying again while she and Janey helped Mother clear away the table. When they finished, Mother put her arm around Marge's shoulders once more.

"Now don't start worrying," she said quietly. "I know you'll do all right."

But Marge continued to worry until Friday night. She was glad there was nothing for the Chamber of Commerce boys and girls to do while they waited for Dr. Tozian. Rod had brought the evening issue of *The Clarion*.

"I suppose you all saw it," he said, spreading the paper out with his one good hand. "A modern factory building with a landscaped yard and parking lot, and a baseball diamond. An artificial lake for power. This X-Ello Corporation—that's its name you know—is offering Eastfield $400,000 for the land."

"Do you suppose any of the money could be used for a new school?" Marge asked, walking over to where he sat and peering over his shoulder, although she had seen the paper at home. She was wondering whether he would say anything to her tonight about his unusual disappearance earlier in the week. Perhaps they could walk together now.

Dr. Tozian's appearance brought her wandering thoughts back to the evening's plan and she repeated her inquiry to him, since none of the students had ventured an answer.

"That's a question we'll have to explore," he said while he counted off the sixteen boys and girls. "Everybody's here; let's get started."

They followed the eager young teacher down a tree-lined street in the fading light of early evening, Bill Tanner walking with him, the others straggling behind. Robins hopped about on the grassy lawns they passed, red squirrels raced and chattered noisily up tree trunks and along leaf-enfolded branches. Now and then a few college students passed them, busily discussing campus affairs while they strolled back to the college grounds, quite oblivious of the little high school group.

The Chamber of Commerce students were equally absorbed in their own affairs—an exciting new experience for Eastfield.

"I suppose Bill's father isn't in favor of the sale," Marge said in a quiet voice to Rod as she fell into step beside him.

"He gets all the law practice there is now," Rod replied significantly.

Just at that moment a bright blue hot-rod tore past them, down the middle of the street. It was a car Marge had never seen before, fast and flashy, stripped of top and fenders. There were a few boys in Eastfield who raced in the controlled segment of the old road near Andover City, now in dis-use by regular traffic and regulated by the State Police, but none had such a car.

"Pretty fancy job," she commented. "Was that Jerome at the wheel?"

"It went by too fast," Rod hedged. "We'll see more new cars if the X-Ello sale goes through." Then, in a confidential tone and changing the subject, "I don't think Dr. Tozian has the low-down on tonight's meeting. Bill has, though."

"What do you mean?" Marge felt like a conspirator. She looked around her at the men and women near by, and at the people driving past. They all seemed harassed.

"Alexander Dodd doesn't want the land sold, and one way or another he controls most of the aldermen," Rod explained. "You know how. One works in his bank and two work for Brundage, and another fellow's boss owes the bank so much money that Old Man Dodd could put him out of business. They'll all vote not to sell. So everybody in town who wants the land sold is going to be here tonight. Some of them are going to try to keep the aldermen from voting against the sale."

"You mean the aldermen know how they're going to vote? Before the offer is read?"

Rodney scoffed at her question. "The mayor got that letter last week, but Shorty didn't find out about it right away. They'd all been told how to vote before he had it in the paper. If he hadn't published the story, it would have been voted down before the people even heard of it!"

It was hard for Marge to believe. It seemed dishonest and the meeting of the aldermen like a rigged television show.

"Mr. Whiting must approve of the sale," she finally ventured. "He wouldn't have let Shorty print the story if he agreed with Mr. Dodd, would he?"

"He's a newspaper man," Rod said and his tone was respectful. "He isn't going to let Old Man Dodd control his paper or suppress news. He's as proud of *The Clarion* as he could be if it were *The New York Times*. So he let Shorty run the story, and the picture tonight, to show Eastfield what the town may lose." He hesitated and his voice dropped even lower. "The people who own houses near Dodd Park, and the vacant lots along the river, would make money on their real estate if we had that factory instead of the old swamp we call Dodd Park!"

They had reached the town hall yard. The other people had stopped talking, and so did the students. The sharp yipping of a small dog, the evening chirps of English sparrows, scuffling feet on sidewalk and pavement were the only sounds. Marge felt her throat tighten when she looked into the sober faces around her, and the crowds pressing near the two-story red brick house with a one-story lean-to, the original Dodd home. She saw Mr. Matthews on the porch railing. Dr. Tozian waved the students back and pushed through the crowd to Mr. Matthews' side. In a moment he returned to them.

"Mr. Matthews suggests you stay together at this end of the yard, under the big maple tree," he said quietly. "You won't be able to see, but perhaps you can hear. He will make room for me up on the porch and I'll report back to you. Can I depend on you?"

They nodded, awed into silence by the tenseness of the crowd. Dr. Tozian looked at his students earnestly. Was he sorry he had brought them? Was he doubtful they would behave, or was there something more serious about this meeting than he had anticipated?

Nearby Marge saw Jerome's father talking earnestly to Mrs. Clarke, the gift shop proprietress.

"All figuring on new fronts for their stores, and how to make Eastfield look like a honky-tonk," Bill muttered to no one in particular. Marge turned to see what answer Rod might have to that remark.

Rod was not in sight! Without a word or a noticeable movement he had vanished!

Dr. Tozian had told his Chamber of Commerce students to stay together, and already Rod had disappeared. Had Bill noticed? She turned her attention quickly to the bare windows of the town hall, hoping no one else would discover that Rod was gone. Overhead lights from an ornate chandelier in the meeting room which once had been a fashionable drawing room, gleamed brightly. Shadows from the big trees wavered on the people outside.

Where was Rod? Why had he left the group when Dr. Tozian had told them to stay together? Her uneasiness was increasing when he did not return.

Suddenly she remembered that blue car. Was Jerome one of the boys riding in it when it sped past them? Had Rod slipped away to join his friend?

Inside a gavel banged on a bare wooden table, chairs scraped and the last coughs quieted. A resonant voice began reading the important letter. People on the porch crammed against the windows, people on the lawn pressed closer to the porch. There wasn't a whisper while the reading went on, but as soon as the sonorous voice ceased, a murmur spread through the crowd. At first Marge couldn't sense its meaning. It was an inarticulate jumble. Then came the words: "Somebody's got to speak up! Say something!"

Marge found herself pressed between Bill and Mr. Chamberlin. Mrs. Clarke had stepped back to the obscurity of the farther trees in the yard.

"Why doesn't somebody speak up?" Mr. Chamberlin demanded. "They'll railroad the sale through to defeat if somebody doesn't say something!"

"Hush! The mayor's talking!"

64

The next voice from inside the town hall was distinct, and Marge heard most of what the mayor said.

"The citizens of Eastfield have shown such an unexpected interest, if anyone wishes to take the floor he may address the chair."

There was a moment's silence and Marge stood on tip-toe trying to see what was happening, hoping someone would speak for the crowd outside town hall.

"If no one has anything to say for the record . . ." There was a slight pause, then the mayor continued ". . . the clerk will proceed with the roll call."

"That's it," Mr. Chamberlin said boldly. "They're railroading the sale out!"

"No! No, they can't do that!" It was being shouted from all sides of the yard.

"Why doesn't somebody address the chair?" Marge heard her own voice groaning.

"There's no leadership here," a fellow student answered.

The rumble was rising to noisy shouts of "No! No!" Then above the voice inside and the clamouring outside, Marge heard Dr. Tozian's voice, bold and challenging.

"Your honor, Mr. Mayor!"

He had left the railing and pushed his way to the window.

"Mr. Mayor!" The voice inside and the hubub outside subsided.

Could Dr. Tozian prevent this action that had been planned in advance by the most important man in Eastfield?

"I have lived in Eastfield only a month, but I have bought my home and I expect to live here a long time," the teacher began. "I do not know enough about the proposed sale to express an opinion, but I respectfully request that the motion to reject the offer be laid on the table until the citizens of Eastfield can become informed and can express their views to the aldermen who represent us."

Shouts of "Yes, that's right," followed Dr. Tozian's proposal.

65

"Make that a motion," came the demand from the people in the yard. They began shouting the names of their aldermen with the admonition, "Don't vote it down tonight."

Marge couldn't hear what was going on inside now, but against the lighted window Dr. Tozian's slender figure stood out and he extended his hands palms downward toward the excited people below him. Gradually they quieted.

"A motion has been made to table it," he explained. "Listen for the vote."

Marge heard a succession of "Ayes," then the mayor's voice saying, "Motion has carried."

Exclamations of relief were followed by a burst of applause. Dr. Tozian jumped over the porch railing and pushed his way toward the tree where he had left his students, Mr. Matthews following. Then, above the excited voices came the startling crash of glass and shouts of surprise and anger inside the building.

"What happened?" It was on everybody's lips. "What happened?"

Shorty appeared in the window and stopped long enough to explain to the crowd.

"Someone just threw a stone through a rear window but nobody's cut or hurt."

Panic gripped Marge as she saw Shorty jump to the ground, following Dr. Tozian and Mr. Matthews to the group of students. She gripped the trunk of the tree weakly and as she did it, rough leather scraped her hand. Down from the low-hanging branches came Rodney, and her heart beat again.

"Rod, were you there all the time?" she gasped. "How did you get there?"

"Bill gave me a boost," he explained. "Somebody had to see what was going on."

Bill! What a relief! "Were you high enough to see over the lean-to?" she asked.

"Don't ever ask me," he whispered. He was looking past her, straight at Shorty.

"This may undo all the good we've done," Mr. Matthews said to Dr. Tozian, "even though all of our boys and girls are here." He wiped his perspiring forehead and sighed audibly.

"Nothing worse could have happened," Shorty said, but he wasn't speaking to Dr. Tozian or Mr. Matthews. His eyes were questioning Rod.

CHAPTER VI

A RED CONVERTIBLE

FOR A FEW minutes Dr. Tozian's High School Chamber of Commerce was the focal point in the town hall yard. Townspeople turned from the building, angry aldermen pushed their way out, the chief of police had appeared on the scene, and all looked at the students suspiciously. Of the sixteen there were only two girls besides Marge—juniors whom she knew as "the Digbee twins." They asked Dr. Tozian if they could go home and hurried to the sidewalk as soon as he said yes. Then Shorty and a younger man who had come out of the building with him, questioned the boys. Did they know anything about the stone-throwing episode? Had it been planned?

Shorty introduced his companion as the Andover City radio station reporter.

"How many of you left the front yard?" the man shot at them. There was an immediate and indignant denial that anyone had left the spot where Dr. Tozian had told them to remain.

"Who threw the stone?" the chief of police demanded.

Again the denial that anyone knew. Marge wanted to look at Rod but feared that even a glance in his direction might focus attention on him—the only one who might know. For a frightened moment she wondered if Bill would tell that he had helped Rod up into the tree from where he might have seen what happened. If the thought came to Bill's mind, he too protected Rod from the inquisitors.

Marge wanted to ask if she could go home, but it was difficult to interrupt. No one was paying any attention to her and she felt alone and strange and almost frightened.

"Aren't you Dr. Ragland's daughter?" a quiet voice beside her asked. The gift shop proprietress was smiling at her. "I'm Mrs. Clarke. Would you like to walk home with me?"

"Yes, I would," Marge said gratefully. "Thank you."

Mrs. Clarke wanted companionship too, Marge thought as she watched the woman rather timidly touch Dr. Tozian's arm to get attention. She motioned in Marge's direction, Dr. Tozian nodded, then Marge and Mrs. Clarke left the crowded lawn and started toward Main Street. It was dark now and street lamps cast patches of light and shadow on the sidewalk and old brick pavement.

"That was awful, wasn't it?" Marge said. "Do you think anyone really believes one of us did it? No one left the front lawn."

"I know you didn't," Mrs. Clarke reassured her. "I could see you all the time. It must have been some youngster, though. Kids have been throwing stones since the Stone Age, I guess. Only it's too bad. Now the aldermen will have another reason for voting against the sale. They'll say five hundred more families would bring problem children, and we've never had any serious juvenile delinquency in Eastfield."

"You're in favor of selling, aren't you?" Marge asked.

"All of the merchants are," Mrs. Clarke replied. "Most of us just barely keep going. Some have to borrow at the bank to get through the slack period in summer when so many families are at the lake. A thriving industry would make all the difference in the world!"

"Did you always have a gift shop?" Marge was thinking of the display she had seen in the window of the little store, while Mrs. Clarke explained how she had started the business after her husband died.

"Where did you get the plastic things I've seen in your window?" Marge asked when they reached Mrs. Clarke's shop.

Mrs. Clarke named the firm. "I had an awful time getting them," she said. "Big manufacturers don't want to make small sales."

"But there are small manufacturers," Marge suggested. "I've read about one."

"If you mean the story in *The Clarion* last spring, I read it too," Mrs. Clarke said. "After the publicity came out, the girl couldn't make things fast enough. I know, for I wrote to her."

"If anyone in Eastfield could make things like that, you could buy them and sell them in your shop, couldn't you?"

"Yes, if they were good," Mrs. Clarke agreed.

"I wanted a plastics course at school, or at least a club for after school," Marge began when rapid footsteps behind them distracted her. She and Mrs. Clarke turned in time to see Mr. Chamberlin almost run across the deserted street to his store, unlock the door and turn on the bright overhead lights. Without stopping to close the door behind him he rushed to the workshop at the back. A blaring radio bellowed into the night and at the same instant Marge saw Jerome. He was sitting at his father's workbench, feet on a table, smoking a cigaret and listening to the music.

Involuntarily Marge heaved a sigh of relief. "I hope he's been there all the time," she said.

"So do I," Mrs. Clarke agreed. "His father seems like a good, hard-working man." She hesitated and Marge wondered if she was remembering the newspaper that had struck her in the face. "How is the boy doing in school?" she asked.

"He isn't in any of my classes," Marge hedged. She didn't want to tell Mrs. Clark that Jerry had refused to play on the football team, and had missed classes, and had failed to be at the newspaper office to meet his obligation there. Could he possibly have had anything to do with tonight's affair? Marge feared that the idea had occurred to Mrs. Clarke too, but the subject of Jerome was not pressed further.

"Here's your street," Mrs. Clarke said quietly. "It's only half a block to your house. You're not afraid here, are you?"

Marge thanked her and said good night. Some other time she would talk to Mrs. Clarke about making things of plastics. Now she wanted to hurry home and tell everyone about the meeting. She was sure neither Mother nor Dad, nor even Janey, had expected anything so unforeseen as this night had brought.

Marge knew the minute she stepped into the hall that the story had preceded her. Mrs. Brundage was in the living room, sitting erect on the davenport, and Mother and Dad were listening to her intently while her fingers tapped indignantly against an alligator bag in her lap.

"Just who is this Dr. Tozian?" she demanded and her tone implied disapproval.

Marge hesitated for a moment then started for the stairs. She wanted to tell about the crowd, and how Dr. Tozian had spoken for the people outside town hall, and the unfortunate climax of her first civic meeting, but not with Mrs. Brundage present. To her surprise, it was Mrs. Brundage who stopped her.

"Oh, Marge, your father's just told me you're one of the new High School Chamber of Commerce members," she said with a condescending smile. "How was the meeting?"

Mrs. Brundage spoke pleasantly enough, but her sharp features seemed more severe than ever. Marge looked at her mother hoping for some opportunity to escape.

"This was Marge's introduction to local government," Mother said quietly. "She hasn't any experience to help her judge the meeting, Mrs. Brundage."

"That's right," her father agreed, emptying his pipe in a convenient ash tray. "We'd like to hear what you saw and heard though, if you want to tell us."

There wasn't any getting out of it. She made it as brief as she could and did not keep anything back, even to the stone that was hurled through the window.

"That probably was the best thing that could have happened." Mrs. Brundage sounded decisive. "It demonstrated what my brother said in the first place. An undesirable element already is crowding into Eastfield. We've kept it a good, clean town all these years. Almost no crime. No narcotics problem. But this fall! Where did all these new people come from? And when? Two platoons at school, . . ."

Dad didn't answer her. "Were you able to see or hear any of the proceedings?" he asked. "We've heard there was a crowd filling the front yard and shouting."

Marge nodded. "Most of the storekeepers were there. I guess they favor the sale. We couldn't even get near the porch. I walked home with Mrs. Clarke and . . ."

Mrs. Brundage interrupted her with a wave of the hand, and just in time. In another minute she would have told them what Mrs. Clarke had said, and perhaps Mrs. Clarke was one of those who had to borrow in the summer from Alexander Dodd's bank.

"Thanks, Marge," Dad said. "Run along and do your homework. There'll probably be a report on the 10:30 news from Andover City."

He picked up his pipe and began refilling it. Relieved, Marge said good night and started for the hall, just as the doorbell gave four short tingles—Carol's signal. Her friend burst into the hall, questions popping.

"What happened? Tell me before I perish with curiosity. Did someone really throw a stone or something? Pops came

72

home with another alderman and . . ." Then she saw Mrs. Brundage and subsided with a confused "Oh!"

"Come on up to our room," Marge said hurriedly, leading the way.

Janey was waiting there, scarcely less eager than Carol. Her eyes shone with excitement and her hair hung in unbrushed disarray against her dark brown pajamas.

"You really got into something, didn't you?" she asked as soon as Marge closed the door. "Hello, Carol. Sit down." She tossed the big velvet cushions from her bed onto the floor for all of them. "What do you know about it? Your father's an alderman."

"All I know is the telephone began ringing before he got home," Carol told them breathlessly. "He and some other men came in and went to the kitchen, shutting the door. But the phone kept on ringing and Mom told me to go up-stairs to bed. It's too early for that, and anyway I'm dying to know what happened."

Marge was glad to tell the whole story at last. She felt proud of Dr. Tozian. He was the one who had kept the aldermen from rejecting the offer.

"The aldermen were really going to turn it down?" Carol gasped. "They want Eastfield to stay a third-rate whistle stop? After the picture in the paper tonight?"

"Alexander Dodd tells everyone on the Board of Aldermen how to vote," Marge said.

"Did Rod tell you that?" Carol demanded. "Shorty knows everything, doesn't he? Does he know who threw the stone?"

"I don't think so," Marge answered.

"Where was Jerry, that's what I'd like to know," Carol went on. "Lois said he wasn't in school this morning until time for his woodworking class."

Marge hadn't known that. "He was in the back of his father's shop playing the radio when Mrs. Clarke and I came along. We both saw him," she said.

"He probably had plenty of time to get there ahead of you

and Mrs. Clarke if he was in the fracas at town hall," Carol sniffed. "I wouldn't put anything past him."

"Well, don't go suggesting he did it, or any other of the new kids," Marge warned, lowering her voice. "That's what Mrs. Brundage and her crowd are counting on to get the sale turned down. She practically said so just now. Five hundred new families with one stone-thrower to a family and Eastfield'll be a shambles!"

"They have a point, Marge," Janey broke in. "We don't want Eastfield turned into a . . . a . . ."

She stopped for a word, and Carol spoke up, "No, but we do want a new school. How are we going to keep up with the rest of the world? Honestly, Eastfield's flying with the Wright brothers!"

"And why should newcomers be considered poor citizens just because they're new?" Marge demanded.

Janey shook her head, obviously disagreeing with the two younger girls. "What we should do is concentrate on supporting Superintendent Griffin," she said emphatically. "He'll be working for a new school and people will respond. We have PTA leaders for all of our clubs already. Bill's father is going to coach Debate Club! But we don't know enough about this X-Ello company to talk about selling them Dodd Park, or thinking that will solve our school problem."

"Then you're against it!" Carol's voice was sharp and Marge felt her spirits drop. Janey must believe their father opposed the industrial development.

"Yes, I'm against it," Janey said decisively. "I don't think the students should get involved, either. Some things are for adults to decide."

Marge didn't want to meet the inquiring look on Carol's face. She and Carol were in the same position—favoring a development that promised a bright, new world while their fathers opposed it. Carol and she would have to keep their feelings to themselves.

74

Janey turned on the radio and the three girls listened to the brief account which was all the Andover City station had time to give. They knew more than the announcer had to tell. When it was over, a subdued Carol went home.

Marge learned the next day, when the newsboy tossed the paper into the yard, that there were other fathers in the ranks of those who opposed the sale. She turned from the front page account of the meeting to read Shorty's column on the inside, but a letter to the editor stopped her.

"POLITICAL BRAWL NO PLACE FOR CHILDREN"

That would be an attack on Dr. Tozian, she knew instantly as she read the sentences that followed the customary "Dear Editor."

> "I cannot imagine what our school officials are thinking of when they not only allow 14 and 15 year old girls to attend a political pow-wow but actually take them to it. What happened in Eastfield last night was a disgrace. Men and women stomping in the town hall yard, and an unknown rowdy hurling a stone through the window of our municipal building. The situation not only brought out the worst in people, but was physically dangerous."

Marge glanced at the signature. The letter was written by John Digbee, father of the Digbee twins. There was more. Marge read it, folded the paper and propped it against the door. She didn't want to be around when Dad read it. She would go to the library or someplace and stay away until dinner time.

She walked along Jewett Avenue until she had passed the last house and the sidewalk merged into a pebbled path. Vacant lots were filled with goldenrod and rich orange-red butterfly weed. She loved the bright clusters of flowers, each tiny bloom reminding her of a fluted vase. She began gathering a bouquet to take home. Around the side of the hill she went, close by the highway leading to Andover City. The whiz of automobiles came to her ears, and the chug of a truck straining uphill. Straightening, she watched the line of traffic all headed toward Andover City.

Then up the hill came a flame of red, swinging around the truck in a burst of easy speed. It was a red convertible which she had never seen before, and crowded in the front seat with the driver were Jerry and Rod!

CHAPTER VII

THE RUSTLE OF TAFFETA

THE NOISY, LAUGHING boys did not see Marge. They were going too fast for her to be sure whether the driver was one of the two who had been with Jerry in the blue hot-rod the night of the nearly disasterous meeting at town hall.

Where were they going now? Why was Rod making Jerry his special friend? Because of the cars she surmised, and the opportunity to get away from sleepy Eastfield. At least the boys had taken care of their work at the newspaper office today before dashing out of town, for the Ragland's paper had been delivered on time. She wouldn't see Rod again until Monday, but she could use today's event as an opening in order to ask a few questions when she did see him.

It was probably time to go home, but ahead she spied a cluster of blue flowers beside a rough wagon trail leading to an apple orchard. Bristol asters were just the thing to go with her butterfly weed. She would gather enough to fill the big green jardiniere in the hall at home.

Her back to the highway and her mind still on Rod, Marge began gathering the flowers. Half consciously she realized that autumn blooms never had the sweet fragrance of spring and summer blossoms. But it was not the flowers she was thinking of, nor did she pay any attention to the traffic behind her, until a persistent honking and a man's voice brought her back to reality.

"Hey, Miss, step aside, will you? You're almost in the middle of the road."

Startled, Marge drew back into the open field. A small truck passed her and came to a halt a few feet farther on. In the back a farmer was standing, holding up some boards which had been nailed together. She knew him as Edwin McGovern, the aging owner of the orchard where her father often bought apples in the fall.

"Hello, Mr. McGovern," she called. "I'm Marge Ragland. Don't you remember me?"

"Sure I remember you," he replied. "It's just these bad old eyes of mine."

The truck driver jumped out and walked to the rear of his car. "Hand it down, steady like," he called. "Show me where you want it put."

Marge watched while Mr. McGovern pushed a small billboard down to the younger man. When they swung it around, big black letters on a light blue background with a bright red border announced building lots for sale.

"You're going to sell lots out here?" Marge asked Mr. McGovern.

"Going to try," the farmer told her, blinking his pale blue eyes. "If Eastfield sells Dodd Park, the new X-Ello people will have to build somewhere. If they don't want to build out here, where there's no sewers and such, then I'll have to sell the orchard, I guess."

He took one end of his gaudy billboard and gestured to the place fronting the highway where he wanted it set up. Marge followed, holding her flowers in her arms.

"Why would you have to sell the orchard?" she asked.

"Can't see to sort and grade apples any more," Mr. Mc-Govern explained. "It'll be all I can do to pick 'em this fall. After I have an operation they say I'll see all right, but I don't know. I'm getting old."

Marge felt sorry for him. She watched for a few moments while he helped get his sign settled securely, then she started home. By now her father would have left his office at the college and had time to read the paper. She dreaded seeing him.

When she entered the front hall she could hear his voice through the open door of his study and she knew he was talking to someone on the telephone. She arranged her orange and blue clusters in the jardiniere, waiting until he came out. He had the paper in his hand.

"Did you see this, Marge?" He gestured with the paper.

Marge looked up from her flowers. "I'm supposed to be the 14-year-old girl, I guess," she said dolefully. "The Digbee twins are past fifteen and we're the only girls in the group. I didn't suppose I looked so young." She glanced at herself in the hall mirror.

"Tell me who the others are again," her father said. "I've just been talking to Superintendent Griffin. He says they're an outstanding group of students and he has complete confidence in them. Besides, there were two faculty members at the meeting and Eastfield citizens don't engage in brawls, either."

Relieved, Marge named her fellow students, glad to be able to include Rod.

"Don't let this article disturb you," he said. "Maybe the Digbee girls were unduly frightened and gave their father the wrong impression." He tossed the paper onto the hall table. "That's a pretty bouquet you've arranged for us," he added. "There's a touch of autumn in the house now."

Marge felt a warm glow of happiness. Dad had understood and had not felt she had put the family in a bad light again.

Now was the time to ask him what he had thought of Rod. But it was hard to begin.

"Dad . . . Now that you've met him—Rod, I mean—and you know what Superintendent Griffin thinks, could I go for a ride with him if he should ever ask me? Not that he has."

Her father hesitated before answering. "If it's a date, let your mother or me know before you go," he said. "The one time I saw Rod he was trying to do the right thing. And Superintendent Griffin thinks Dr. Tozian's group are a fine lot of students."

"I don't think he'd drive recklessly," Marge said. But she wondered whether he really had good sense. Surely Jerry wasn't acting sensibly, and Rod was seeing him all the time now.

It was the middle of the week before Marge saw Rod alone. She was beginning to think he was avoiding her when she found him at her side after social studies.

"Are you headed for your proofreading job?" he asked.

"Right after lunch," Marge told him. "Are you going down to the office?" It would be fun to walk down Main Street again, perhaps have him check proofs with her.

"I don't know," he answered. "I'm meeting Jerry after woodworking."

Jerry again! Her momentary glow of pleasant anticipation ended abruptly. Marge walked with him toward the woodworking shop, although he hadn't asked her to. It was the end of the morning and the boys were cleaning up their work benches for the afternoon platoon. There was always an odor about the shop of fresh lumber and hot glue and today there was a noisy hum of voices as the session closed.

For an instant Marge and Rod stood in the open door looking for Jerry. Then they heard his voice, clear above the others.

"Watch it, you over there!"

A planer shot half way across the room, landed deftly right side up on one of the workbenches, and slid to a stop directly in front of the tool panel on the wall. Marge caught her breath. It was a skillful throw but if anyone had inadvertently stepped into the path of that flying tool, there would have been a bad accident.

"Who did that?" Mr. Matthews demanded instantly. His gray eyes were dark with indignation.

The noise subsided and Marge and Rod stepped back from the doorway.

"I said at the beginning of this course that there was to be no horseplay," the instructor said severely. "I want to know who threw that planer."

Marge wondered whether Jerry was going to admit his guilt or keep still. When he spoke, his voice was surly.

"You know who did it. I did."

"Any more unsafe practices and you'll be dismissed from this class, and for good," Mr. Matthews said. "You've made the best start on the best piece of work in school, but we don't tolerate any nonsense here. Tools can be dangerous when they aren't properly handled. That's all now."

In silence the boys stacked their tools in neat rows in the wall panels, took off their dark blue work aprons, and left the room. Most of them ignored Jerry. No one waited to walk out of the school shop with him.

Jerry hung his apron on its peg, peered at himself in a small wall mirror, and smoothed his sleek black hair with a pocket comb. Marge wished she had not come with Rod. She would have no opportunity to talk with him now, and she didn't want Mr. Matthews to think she had come seeking Jerome.

No one mentioned his ill-advised stunt when Jerry joined Marge and Rod.

"I thought I'd see whether you are going bowling tonight," Rod said as the three climbed the stairs to the main corridor together.

"If I can get the car," Jerry replied. "I'll know by the time I get to *The Clarion*."

"Are you two still bowling?" Marge asked.

Jerry took notice of her for the first time.

"And getting the wood," he said. "A turkey for Rod the last time."

Marge frowned. She didn't know what Jerry was talking about. She felt he was deliberately speaking a bowling lingo she did not understand.

"You'll learn," he said as though reading her thoughts. "And as I said once before, you'll make a strike yourself, one of these days."

They had reached the main corridor and when Rod said he'd see his friend later, Jerry dismissed them both with a wave of the hand.

"I don't see what you find to like in him," Marge said as she and Rod started for the lunchroom.

"I don't suppose you do," Rod answered a little gruffly. "That's the whole trouble. But who is counting out papers for me? Who's taking my route, and not asking to keep the job when I get out of this thing?" He grimaced at his bandaged arm. "You know how many jobs there are for kids in Eastfield. His dad hasn't enough business at the new shop to keep busy himself."

"I guess Jerry delivers your papers when he gets there," Marge retorted.

"He's been there every time but once," Rod said and offered no explanation of the time when neither boy had appeared to take charge of the newsboys.

"I suppose you were going bowling when you breezed by me in the red car Saturday afternoon," Marge went on.

"Where were you?" Rod asked, evading an answer.

"Out on the highway where Mr. McGovern was putting up his real estate sale sign," she told him.

"His what?"

"Sign. Billboard. He didn't have it up when you and Jerry and the other fellow tore past," Marge explained. "I suppose it was dark when you got back."

82

Rod ignored the implied question. "Tell me more," he said. "What's the sign say?"

Marge told him all she knew.

"And it's been there since Saturday and Shorty hasn't heard a thing about it? Excuse me, Marge. I still have to live with the guy."

She watched him streak across the street, looking one way and then the other for traffic, and she knew he was going to telephone Shorty.

With a feeling that she had been abandoned, and the shadow of her near quarrel with Rod darkening her mood, Marge started for the lunchroom. Perhaps Carol and Lois were meeting there as they frequently did. She saw the sisters in the cafeteria line and made her way to them.

"Pick up a glass of milk and a tuna sandwich for me, and I'll get a table for us," she told Carol, handing over her money. "With lettuce and tomato and mayonnaise on rye."

When the girls joined her they were excitedly planning a shopping trip to Andover City after school.

"Mom's going to drive us over," Carol said. "Want to go too? There are dress sales at two stores there and we thought now would be a good time to get something for the Harvest Hop. There's nothing at Dolly's Dress Shoppe here. We've looked."

Marge wanted to go, but she didn't have a date for the Hop. Maybe it was foolish to buy a dress before she had a date.

"I'll call Mother before I go down to *The Clarion* and see where she has charge accounts. I haven't enough money with me, of course," Marge admitted. "Have you both got dates for the Hop? I might as well admit I haven't. Maybe I shouldn't buy a dress when I haven't a date."

"This first party is 'Girl Dates Boy,' don't you remember?" Carol reminded her. "The next one is 'Boy Dates Girl.' We voted to start alternating a year ago. Social equality or some-

83

thing. The committee'll probably have a notice on the bulletin board in another day or two. Maybe Janey has something in the school paper. Don't you know?"

Marge didn't know. She had taken the copy to Shorty as usual but she hadn't read it all. She would have to read proof today.

When Marge called her mother she found that the Raglands had charge accounts at both of the stores Carol had mentioned. It was the first time Marge had ever picked out a party dress alone, and the idea was exciting.

Exciting too was the idea that she might ask some boy instead of waiting to be invited. "Some boy?" What boy was there to invite except Rod? She thought of the other boys in her classes. Bill Tanner's brother Lewis? She had an idea Carol was going to invite Lewis.

Marge read the proofs with more than usual interest, watching for the announcement of the Harvest Hop. It was there, with the list of committee members and the name of the band that had been engaged. There was a reminder, too, that girls were to ask boys for this first party.

"Any bright, new ideas for the Hop, anyone? Let's make this party different in more ways than just 'Girl Dates Boy.'"

Marge didn't have any bright ideas. She waited until she saw Jerry arrive to count out the newsboys. He came without Rod, so she left at once to meet Carol and Lois and their mother.

Long rows of party frocks in the Andover stores were as thrilling as she had anticipated. Against the wall were the more expensive dresses and on racks in the middle of the showroom were the "mark downs." Most of them were much too formal for an Eastfield school dance.

Blue sequins sparkled on rose tulle. Beaded rosebuds trailed over a billowing green skirt. White brocade with a scarlet belt. Sophisticated black. One by one Marge pushed them back along the rack. These would never do.

Carol and Lois left the bargains to look at the higher priced new dresses in alcoves along the wall and Marge was about to follow them when her hand automatically pushed the next dress forward. It was blue, her favorite color. Beneath a soft overskirt, pleated taffeta rustled alluringly. The neck was high with a binding of pearls. Mother would approve of this for it was feminine and demure. When she tried it on, it fitted perfectly but she sought out Carol, needing approval.

"Darling!" Carol exclaimed. "It makes your eyes look practically periwinkle."

That did it. Marge knew her deep blue eyes with their frame of long lashes were her most attractive feature. But before she made the decision to buy, she pirouetted down the aisle between rows of pale pink fitting rooms to find Lois. How soft the material was against her bare arms and shoulders. She loved that dress!

Marge found the younger girl slumped in a chair, hair dishevelled and wearing only a slip, while she waited for her mother to find another dress to try. Lois brightened at the sight of Marge.

"It's pretty and it fits you!" Lois exclaimed. "I found one I like, but by the time we pay for alterations Mom says it will be too much. That's always the way it is for Carol and me. If we could only sew we could fix these things!"

Marge felt sorry for her, even while she was delighted with her own good fortune. She found the sales lady, took off the blue dream cloud, and got back into her brown jacket and skirt once more.

Carol and Lois looked in another store, then another. Waiting, her precious gold and blue striped box propped in her lap as she sunk into an over-sized chair, Marge's mind wandered from the memory of a swishing blue skirt to the Hop. She would have to ask Rod now. When? As soon as the school paper came out? And where was Rod now? Over here in Andover City somewhere with Jerry, probably, because there was no place in Eastfield to bowl. No place where Carol and Lois could learn to sew. No plastics course so she could enter the Industrial Arts Award competition too.

Why didn't someone point up all these things, so people would see what Eastfield needed? The students grumbled but not one did anything. Why couldn't they do something themselves? Perhaps write a whole series of articles for their own school paper about the school they wanted? She knew what she wanted. Carol and Lois knew. Rod knew. Maybe the Digbee girls and others had ideas, too.

Suddenly the plan took shape and seemed really terrific. Perhaps she could schedule the series herself. Maybe this would be her "strike."

But would Janey go along with the idea?

Better not say anything about it, even to Carol and Lois, until she could talk with Janey.

CHAPTER VIII

HARVEST HOP INVITATION

MARGE COULD scarcely wait to get home with her dress box and her idea. Mother had put a casserole of potatoes and ham into the oven and the delicious smell filled the kitchen and back hall. Janey had finished setting the table when Marge came in.

"I hope you'll both like it," Marge called to them. "Come into the living room and see, can't you?" She dropped her purse on the davenport, hastily opened the box, held the lovely blue dress against her, and looked eagerly for approval when her mother and Janey came in. At first neither one spoke.

"But Marge," Janey began, then stopped.

"It's a lovely shade of blue," Mother said. "I like the way it's made." Then she stopped too and Marge knew something was wrong.

"What's the matter?" she asked, draping the rustling dress across the back of the davenport. "It fits perfectly and it was only $9.95. Carol and Lois both paid more."

"But Marge, I'm afraid it's a summer dress," Mother said kindly. "That's why it was marked down."

"Oh! You mean it won't be right for the Harvest Hop?" Marge could have wept.

"It's a real bargain, dear," Mother conceded, touching the material lightly. "I wonder if we could make it look like a fall dress if we introduced some darker shade of blue velvet some way. What do you think, Janey?"

"I think we should take it back," Janey said decisively.

"But we can't take it back," Marge almost sobbed. "All sales were final." She turned to hide the tears that were ready to drop from her lashes.

"Don't be so heartbroken," Mother admonished. "I think we can do something. If any of us knew how to sew we might make a velvet over-jacket."

The suggestion gave Marge an opening.

"That's just what Lois was saying," she reported. "If we had a real home economics course probably Janey and I could both have learned how to make velvet flowers or something. All we have is cooking one semester and how to make slips and aprons the next! And Janey, I had an idea this afternoon while I was waiting for the girls to find dresses that would fit them. You probably won't think much of that either," she added, still hurt and unhappy.

"Don't start feeling sorry for yourself," Janey said. "What's the big idea?"

"Well, so many kids know what they wish we had in school, why don't we write a series of articles for the school paper? We've got to have a new school of some sort. Why can't we at least say what we'd like?"

"It is an idea," Janey admitted. "I wonder how it would work out. I'd like to know we were going to have a real series, with good suggestions. . . ."

It wasn't much encouragement, but it was more than Marge had dared hope for.

"I could line up the stories and writers in advance," Marge

offered. "I know what I want. Lois wants advanced dressmaking and even tailoring. Carol wishes we had organized dramatics with real stage properties and dressing rooms and lights."

"What about the boys?" Janey asked.

"Rod wants electronics and he knows what the other boys are talking about," Marge said. "Radio astronomy . . . microminiaturization. . . . Jerry knows about the shops and equipment they have at Andover City. I don't know whether Rod could get him to write. . . ."

"Why don't you girls go upstairs and put the dress away, and talk it over," Mother suggested. "It's almost time Dad came home for dinner."

Marge gathered together the box with its tissue paper and her dress and followed Janey to their room. She didn't want her father to see another of her mistakes just now.

"You know, Marge, the more I think of this idea of yours, the better I like it," Janey said, opening the closet door and making room for the new dress in a plastic garment bag. "I'll have to clear it with Superintendent Griffin so don't say anything to the girls or to Rod until I know we can do it. You could be working on your own article this weekend if you want to. I'll write an Editor's Note to introduce it. We'll have that to show him on Monday."

Marge's spirits rose. "I'll make a list of all those I know who have ideas they could write about," she promised.

By Monday morning Marge and Janey each had their material ready to submit to the superintendent, and Monday night Janey had his endorsement of the series.

Marge was delighted. She would ask Rod to write about the electronics course right away. It would give her a reason for seeking him out after social studies and maybe she could invite him to be her date for the Hop. Somehow Mother would do something about the dress, so it would be all right.

But Rod once more headed for the woodworking shop after social studies, and Marge was not going there again. She ate lunch with the girls, scheduled two more articles for the school paper, and started for the newspaper office alone, wondering when and how she would see Rod.

Half way down Main Street the screaming horn and clamoring bell of the town's fire truck startled her. Shoppers left the stores to look up and down, automobiles increased speed, and the street was suddenly filled with people.

"Where's the fire?" The question was asked over and over.

"The engine's stopped down in the next block," a tall clerk from one of the stores said, stretching his thin neck to see over the heads of others less tall.

Marge could glimpse the red fire truck through a curtain of automobiles which all but barred it from sight. The siren on the police chief's car blew an insistent warning as he sped past other traffic to the scene.

Was the cloud of smoke that now billowed into the street coming from Mrs. Clarke's gift shop or Mr. Chamberlin's new store? Behind her came the thud of running feet and Rod dashed up.

"I think it's Jerry's place," he panted. "Hurry if you want to come with me."

She quickened her pace to keep up with him, suddenly apprehensive.

"Where's Jerry?" she asked. "Did you see him after woodworking?"

"He wasn't there today," he told her, his voice serious. She glanced at him and saw his thin jaw set, his face strained. Jerry was becoming a truant.

Rod pushed his way through the crowd and Marge followed. The acrid smell of smoke stung her nostrils and brought tears to her eyes. Helmeted firemen had the black hose line inside the store and the police chief, severe in his blue uniform, was ordering people off the sidewalk. She was glad to move from the front row of spectators where Rod had forced their way. The town's auxiliary volunteer fire fighters were assembling on the sidelines now, distinguished by their red arm bands and ready to form a bucket brigade if the one hose line proved inadequate. With them was Shorty, watching everything, questioning everybody.

"There's Mr. Chamberlin, around at the side," Rod said, coughing and wiping his eyes with the back of his hand. Marge saw Shorty leave the line of volunteers and go to the store owner. "He's got the records, it looks like. Ledger books and stuff, I guess. And there's Jerry," Rod added, sounding relieved.

The police chief as well as Shorty hurried toward Mr. Chamberlin. Jerry stood alone for a moment, his face dark, scowling and smoke-stained. Rod gestured and he made his way to the place where Marge and Rod stood, near the gift shop.

"How did it happen?" Rod asked at once, and Marge echoed his words.

"It was my fault, but I didn't set it, if that's what you're thinking," Jerry said. "I don't care if it burns to the ground!" The old bitterness sounded in his voice.

"What do you mean?" Rod asked. "How did it happen?"

"I was in the shop arguing with the old man. He was mad because I didn't get up and go to school this morning. Then we had a rush of customers! Two at once!"

He grimaced sourly and went on with his story.

"Dad told me to get into the shop and help if I wasn't going to school, so I threw my cigaret down and went up front. The next thing we knew the whole back end was full of smoke. If I'd only shut the door behind me this would have been a real good fire. Now they'll put it out and we'll still be in business."

"Jerry! What makes you say such things?" Marge demanded. "They're pulling out the fire hose now. They've put it out and you should be glad."

"Well, I'm not. If we'd burned out we'd have had to move back to Andover, and . . ."

Before Jerry had finished the sentence the police chief walked toward them.

"The fire chief and I want to see you," he said to Jerry. "Over here." He frowned at the crowd of spectators. "Let's break it up! The show is over."

Marge and Rod again moved back and stood at the far side of the gift shop. What questions were being asked of Jerry now, Marge wondered. Surely he was guilty of nothing but carelessness.

"Are you going down to *The Clarion?*" Marge finally asked.

Rod shook his head. "Shorty won't want me under foot. He's headed back to the office now and he'll get a flash about the fire in tonight's paper. You go on, though."

Mention of her assignment brought Marge back to her story in the school paper. She opened the envelope, found Janey's "Editor's Note," and let him read it before showing him her own article. Thoughtfully she scanned it again. But now there was an extra paragraph. "Rule box" it was marked and the copy was signed with the initials of Superintendent Griffin. In a few brief sentences he had estimated what it would cost to introduce a plastics course.

For a moment Marge felt cheated. Janey hadn't told her about this. She handed it all to Rod, almost holding her breath to see what he would say.

"Not bad! Not bad at all," he commented. "You really had an idea this time."

"But this box!" Marge said. "Won't that scare everybody out of writing?"

"It shouldn't," Rod told her. "Everything costs money. Having the facts won't hurt."

"Will you write the next article?" Marge asked. "You know what you want."

"I sure do. More than the electronics shop,'" he said. "Do you know what they have in modern schools now? Electronic classrooms! The kids sit in booths and the teacher sits in the center of the room at the controls. The kids can recite at their own pace and the teacher listens. Helps them individually. If someone is slow, or goofs, the whole class doesn't know about it. But what that would cost! I won't write about that, especially with the rule box coming at the end. He might not be able to figure it!"

"But it's an idea and most of us never heard of such a thing," Marge said. "What we want is good new ideas. Say you'll write about it."

"I'll write about the electronics shop," he promised.

Marge didn't press him. He was thinking about Jerry, she was sure. Rod wasn't slow and didn't goof, but perhaps Jerry had and Rod knew about it. Besides, the electronic classroom did sound like an expensive teaching method and beyond Eastfield. She wasn't sure she would like such isolation and loss of recognition from her classmates when she did well. She was glad to have the assurance Rod would write, and to know he thought her series was a good idea.

"I have something else to ask you," Marge said after a moment's silence.

"Yes?" He leaned against the side of the store, his eyes on the cluster of men still talking to the police chief, the fire chief, Mr. Chamberlin and Jerry.

What an unromantic place to ask him to be her date! Why had she thought this was the time? She didn't respond to his question.

"Yes?" he repeated. "What else?"

There was only one question on her mind. She couldn't think of anything else.

"Will you be my date for the Harvest Hop?"

He stared past her and didn't answer at once.

He hadn't wanted her to ask him! He wanted to say no. She looked away, her cheeks burning. Why had she asked him here and now? Why had she asked him at all?

"Better wait until you find out about the party before you ask me," Rod said at last. "You may not want to go yourself."

"Why not? What do you mean?" Marge asked. There was something evasive about Rod's answer and his manner.

93

"The committee asked for ideas, didn't they?" Rod still avoided looking at her. "Well, I had one. If they buy it . . . I don't know. . . . I think you ought to know about the party first, so let's wait and see."

"I think this is being awfully mysterious," Marge said stiffly but Rod seemed not to hear her. His eyes were on the men who were still questioning Jerry.

"Maybe I'd better go down to *The Clarion*," Marge said. She hoped Rod would change his mind and offer to go with her, but he didn't so she left with the final stragglers who were returning to their own concerns, now that the fire was out and the last wisps of smoke were being blown skyward by the autumn breeze.

What had Rod proposed for the Hop that might make him think she wouldn't want to go, Marge wondered. At least he hadn't said that he had another date. Was there anything about the party in this issue of the school paper?

Marge opened the big brown envelope again and read the headlines on the stories that made up the week's issue. She came to the brief article about the Hop almost at once.

"DO WE HAVE IDEAS?

"So many of them that the Harvest Hop committee can't decide which is best. There'll be a final meeting Wednesday night. Look for a notice on the bulletin board Thursday. And save the date—as though anyone at Eastfield wouldn't."

There wasn't a clue nor a name. She put the papers back in the envelope, being careful not to separate headlines from copy. The toot of an automobile horn beside her failed to distract her. What idea had Rod proposed?

"Hello, beautiful. What are you reading? Love letters?" It was a young man's voice, a smooth, southern drawl.

Marge looked up quickly. The red convertible was moving along slowly beside her, and she had a good look at the driver now. He was older than Rod or Jerry—probably twenty at least, and very good looking. He wasn't dressed in jeans or slacks, but wore a tweed sport suit, and shirt and tie.

"I could take you wherever you're going," he offered. "I'm going there too."

Marge busied herself with her envelope and avoided looking at him. She certainly was not going to be picked up by the fellow who might be connected with Jerry's truancy, and the expeditions he and Rod were making to Andover City more and more frequently.

"You look so nice and friendly," he persisted. "Don't you feel just a little friendly?"

How was she to get away from him? The car was simply crawling along. She would have to go into one of the stores and price something she didn't want and couldn't buy. Of course he could wait outside for her. What should she do?

Behind her she heard running footsteps and the next instant Jerry was jumping into the barely moving car.

"Cut it, Morris," he said sharply. "Let's get out of here."

Morris ignored him, idled the car along, and began singing in a clear tenor.

"Love! I know my moonflower love!"

"Oh, cut it, will you?" Jerry stormed. "That's Rod's girl, and nothing but a kid!"

Rod's girl. So Jerry, Rod's best friend, thought she was Rod's girl. She couldn't admire Jerry and she didn't understand Rod's behavior, but it was a pleasant thought. Except the part about being a kid.

"I'll see you again," the southern voice drawled. "Some time when this uncouth character isn't along. So long for now, honey."

Slowly the car picked up speed. The singing began again. . . . "I know my moonflower love. . . ."

Love! This was the year when Marge had hoped some boy at least would notice her. The only boy she was interested in at all had practically turned down her invitation to the Harvest

95

Hop just a few minutes ago. Love was the farthest thing from Rod's mind, she was sure. And she wasn't exactly thinking about it herself. In spite of all the popular teen-ager's songs, it was a word for something still in the future.

The red car swung around the corner ahead of her and out of sight, probably on the route to Andover City. Was Jerry going to skip his job at *The Clarion* tonight? At least Rod wasn't with him, if he was off on some escapade. Rod's arm would soon be out of the sling, but he could scarcely count out papers tonight. Perhaps she could waste time enough so she would be there when the papers came off the press, and so find out what the boys did. Perhaps she could wait someplace where she could see the alley, but not be conspicuous.

She walked slowly the rest of the way to the newspaper office, stopped to talk to the girl behind the long, high counter stood for a while at the entrance to Shorty's office with her envelope in her hands, instead of depositing it in the wire basket where she always left it. Shorty was reading the proof of his front page again, and once more inch-high type strung across the top of page one.

Could that little fire be worth such a headline, Marge wondered. Was there more to it than she knew?

"Hi, Marge," Shorty said without looking up. "You're in time for a sneak prevue."

At this invitation she walked to his long table, where she could read the banner.

X-ELLO OFFICIALS HERE FOR CITIZENS MEETING

"X-Ello people here!" Marge exclaimed. She had almost forgotten the offer to buy Dodd Park.

"That's it," Shorty told her. "We've got a town committee if we haven't a Chamber of Commerce like the one you high

96

school kids have. And the committee's got the school auditorium booked for an open meeting where people can hear what the X-Ello owners have to say about their offer. Where they can question 'em."

"When did all this happen?" Marge asked, trying to read the column in a glance. "How did it happen?"

"It's been cooking ever since the night of the aldermen's meeting," Shorty told her. "As for how, your Dr. Tozian is chairman of the committee, it says here."

"Does Alexander Dodd know? And Mrs. Brundage?"

"Probably," Shorty admitted. "Somebody always tells them everything. But if this secret has been kept for a change, they'll know it in another ten minutes, when the boys get their papers on the street. You can be sure we're not late today! Mr. Whiting thinks we just might have a real scoop with this story."

CHAPTER IX

HARVEST AND HOP

MARGE STEPPED GINGERLY behind Shorty as he made his way through the shop with its weird blue-purple lights, to the pressroom. His mind was on the alley too, she was sure. If Rod and Jerry were not there, it would be up to Shorty to take off his coat, roll up his sleeves, and once more count out papers for the newsboys.

Jerry was nowhere around, but Rod had come. Marge held back, out of sight.

"Let her roll," Shorty called to the pressman and stepped into the alley.

"Do you blame him?" she heard Rod shout above the slow grinding roar as the press started. "Everybody jumped on him as though he'd set the fire deliberately. I can manage with the help of one of the big boys, I guess. Anyway, I told him I could."

Marge didn't wait. Quickly she made her way back through

the shop, through Shorty's office where the racing tick-tock of his French clock was the only sound, and out to the street.

After dinner that night she watched her father read the evening paper with nervous interest, waiting for his comment about the X-Ello meeting.

"I suppose we should go," he said to her mother. "I don't see how I can spare the time, though. I've a committee meeting at the Capitol that day and I thought you could drive me up, so I could go over the figures again on the way."

"We might still get home in time," Mother suggested. "It is an important meeting."

To Marge it was very important. Her campaign for the school could scarcely succeed if Mr. Dodd and Mrs. Brundage kept Eastfield in its present straight jacket.

In social studies the next day assigned work was practically forgotten. The class crowded around Dr. Tozian at the front of the room.

"Can the Chamber of Commerce go to the X-Ello meeting?" Rod and Marge asked simultaneously. It was foremost on everyone's mind.

Dr. Tozian listened to the questions and discussion, his dark eyes darting from student to student when they spoke. As usual, he made no attempt to divert or control the conversation. With a quick gesture of his long, sensitive hands he hushed the excited voices and when Marge could be heard, she spoke with conviction.

"I think the Chamber of Commerce members have an obligation to attend," she said. "That's the sort of thing we were organized for. My father and mother think it's an important meeting and they're going if they can get home from the Capitol in time."

Mention of Dr. Ragland's interest brought a momentary hush, and to Marge the uncomfortable remembrance that her father hadn't indicated more than a sense of obligation to attend. She hadn't thought the strength of his position might influence anyone, least of all Dr. Tozian who now fixed his attention on her. She was glad Jerry wasn't in this class; she knew what he would say: "VIP's always get what they want!"

Dr. Tozian's reply eased her discomfort. "I'm glad you all think the same way about it, as I judge you do," he said. "If the afternoon platoon makes it unanimous, we'll have a brief Chamber of Commerce meeting at 12:30 tomorrow noon to elect officers. Members who have their parents' consent may go to the citizens' meeting, but Superintendent Griffin wants written notes of consent."

So it had all been thought out and planned in advance! Inwardly Marge heaved a sigh of relief. She was further relieved the next day when a less agitated group met and elected their most serious and responsible member president—Bill Tanner. That made it easier to ask her father for permission to attend—permission which was granted reluctantly, she was sure. He had not forgotten the meeting the students attended at town hall, and the subsequent "Letter to the Editor."

The X-Ello meeting had the entire school talking, but it did not supplant speculation about the Harvest Hop plan which the committee was to make Wednesday night. Thursday morning Marge and almost every other girl and boy hurried to the bulletin board in the main hall. The announcement should be posted there, and it was—a hand-printed sign, done in rust and brown and green inks.

"It's a Harvest And a Hop!

"1:30 p.m. meet at the Edwin McGovern farm for an afternoon's work in the orchard.

"6 to 8 p.m. Weenie roast—all you can eat.

"8 to 11 p.m. Barn dance in the McGovern barn."

There were gasps of astonishment, suppressed groans of disappointment, and an occasional "Swell idea." Then Rod jumped onto a chair near the bulletin board.

"Now hear this!" he began and grinned engagingly. "The Hop committee asked me to do the honors since I've got to confess I'm the responsible guy."

He looked over the quieting group, then went on.

"Most of us know Mr. McGovern. Most of us didn't know until a few days ago that he has cataracts in his eyes and can't see to grade his apples this year. After he has an operation he should be all right. So the idea is that we'll go to the orchard and if he hasn't cleaned the trees thoroughly, we'll pick the rest of his apples. We'll sort them into Grade A and Grade B, or whatever the grading is, and take out the culls for cider. The county agricultural agent will supervise the work, since we haven't any vocational agriculture department here at Eastfield—another idea for your series, Marge," he added, looking directly at her for the first time. "The Hop committee promises all the franks and baked beans and potato salad we can eat. Then we hop!"

With that he hopped down from the chair.

"What about our clothes?" the girls began to inquire. More than one dress had been bought especially for the Harvest Hop, Marge was sure, as she thought of her own blue dress hanging in the plastic bag in the closet, waiting for the touch of velvet that would transform it into a fall creation.

"It won't be formal," Rod called out. "Barn dance clothes, I'd say." He dodged around the edge of the crowd and headed for his first class.

The idea was not immediately popular, but it could not very well be opposed. Marge wondered with considerable indignation why he had thought she might not want to help Mr. McGovern with his harvest. Jerry's idea, she suspected. Jerry with the eternal chip on his shoulder—against everyone and thinking everyone was against him.

She'd certainly squash that idea just as soon as possible. She'd ask Mr. Rodney Maguire to be her date for the Hop the first minute she saw him alone. And if he hedged, this was the kind of party she could attend without a date. It was all right with her she told herself, knowing in her heart that it would be dreadful.

Rod, however, gave her no immediate opportunity to repeat the invitation. After social studies the next day he made a rush for the woodworking class, and when the Chamber of Commerce met in the social studies room in the evening to go to the auditorium he was the last to arrive. Was he trying to avoid her, she wondered. Didn't he want her to repeat her invitation? Perhaps his suggestion that she might not want to go was just his way of declining, without hurting her feelings. She avoided looking in his direction while Bill Tanner counted off the membership after calling the meeting to order. The Digbee girls had not come, she noticed. No one mentioned their absence, nor Mr. Digbee's "Letter to the Editor."

"We don't want anyone to criticize Dr. Tozian for letting us attend," Bill began, and Marge was sure he had that letter in mind too. He stood erect in front of Dr. Tozian's table, his face more serious than usual. "If everyone agrees, we'll go to the auditorium now and take seats in the back row where we'll be as inconspicuous as possible. Let's not do any talking. If somebody must say something to somebody else, write it."

It sounded like good advice. Checking for pencils and scratch paper first, the fourteen students trooped to the auditorium. The stage was bare except for three chairs placed out of range of the motion picture screen.

The auditorium was filling. At the front of the room Superintendent Griffin stood with some of his Board of Education members, watching the early arrivals. Shorty and the Andover City radio man were among the first to appear.

The gathering reminded Marge of the aldermen's meeting at town hall. Faces were serious, men and women talked in hushed voices and looked around them almost surreptitiously as though half defiant, half afraid of being seen there.

Marge watched for her parents who had not returned home by the dinner hour, and for Alexander Dodd and Mrs. Brundage, but by 8 o'clock none of them had arrived. Promptly at that hour Dr. Tozian came onto the stage. He stood quietly, waiting for the coughing and whispering and scuffing of feet to subside.

"The order for the evening calls for motion pictures of X-Ello plants in Cleveland and Indianapolis first," he began. "These are scenes currently filmed which give us an idea of what the company has done elsewhere and what is proposed for Eastfield. Then two representatives of the firm will speak briefly and answer questions. Now if the operators are ready . . ."

"Mr. Chairman!" came an interruption from the floor. Nervous coughing started again.

Dr. Tozian scanned the audience, then recognized Mr. Digbee. Marge stared at the back of his balding head.

"Before the meeting begins I wish to propose a motion. I move that the room be cleared of children."

Marge and her fellow students suppressed gasps and looked at each other in silent confusion. There were gasps from the audience as well, indistinguishable mutterings, and men and women turned in their seats to spot the offending group. Many had not noticed the High School Chamber of Commerce members, quiet in the back row.

"The motion will be entertained, of course, Mr. Digbee," Dr. Tozian said, "but the audience should understand that the high school students, to whom I presume you refer, are here with the written consent of their parents. This is an open meeting for citizens of Eastfield and these young people are young citizens, not children."

Mr. Digbee waved a hand angrily. "I contend this is a propaganda meeting. Adults should be able to analyze it. We can discuss the subject openly after we've seen the pictures— highly glamorized, probably. But immature boys and girls should not be exposed to attempted brainwashing, if I may use the word. I repeat my motion."

In spite of Bill's warning, whispering started in the back row. "What will we do?"

Rod, who was sitting at the end, put his feet against the back of the seat in front of him. "We'll stay right here," he said crossing his arms over his chest.

Bill Tanner shook his head. "We'll go without being ordered out," he directed. "Why put Dr. Tozian on the spot? Why make the audience take sides? Things are bad enough without our making them volcanic."

Rod did not budge as the rest of the students got to their feet, following Bill's leadership.

"Let them out, Rod," Bill ordered. "I mean it, and I'm in charge."

Rod gave Bill a defiant glare, reluctantly got to his feet and stood back, letting the others pass him. Marge wondered if he intended to stay alone, but when it came her turn to file out he stepped into line behind her. When they reached the corridor, he faced Bill.

"You make me sick! We have as much right to be here as Mr. Digbee," Rod declared. "We should have stood our ground."

"And have the meeting turned into a rout before it began?" Bill demanded. "Embarrass Superintendent Griffin and Dr. Tozian? No! Now everybody clear out and go home."

Most of the boys seemed glad to get out of the building but Rod grabbed Marge's arm and held her back. Before she realized what he had in mind he was pulling her along the corridor and down a side hall toward the woodshop. He led the way through a dimly lighted locker room to steps at the back of the stage. There they huddled in semi-darkness and listened. Sweat dampened Marge's forehead and her hands were cold. What if they were discovered?

They could not see the pictures but they could hear the commentary and the burst of applause at the end. Gradually Marge's nervous excitement lessened. She listened intently when the X-Ello officials explained their plans for Eastfield.

Mr. Digbee had not been convinced and he had supporters in the audience who had come forearmed with negative comments and questions intended to embarrass the speakers. In the end Dr. Tozian took the floor and urged calm and considerate planning. He ended with the admonition that unless

Eastfield did plan for its future, expansion would come in an undesirable way.

"Already we have the site for a Shacktown on the road to Andover," he said. "You will see it mushroom in the spring, a rural slum without sewers or lighting or safe water. Take a drive to the west side of Andover and see what has happened there!"

Rod made a startled move. "So the guy gets around," he muttered and got to his feet cautiously.

"What's he talking about?" Marge whispered. "What's a Shacktown? What's there?"

Rod shook his head instead of answering and motioned to her to follow him. Back through the creaking corridors they tiptoed, their steps sounding like a brigade to Marge. But they were out of the building undetected before the meeting ended.

"You'd better let me walk you home," Rod said when they were safely on the street. "It's dark now."

Marge thanked him. "I'm not afraid of the dark, though," she said. "Nor of picking apples, either. Why did you think I wouldn't want to go to your Harvest and Hop?"

It wasn't the defiant way she had intended to ask him again to be her date, but in the soft light flickering through the trees from the street lamps, she no longer felt defiant.

"I didn't think it was the kind of party you had expected," Rod explained. "I didn't know what your father would think of having you sort apples. It's not exactly dainty work, you know. He might put his foot down."

"If the rest of the girls can do it, so can I," Marge told him. "And my father would want me to help Mr. McGovern grade his apples and get them into cold storage. So I'm going, Rod, whether you want to be my date or not."

He took her hand gently. "I want to be your date," he said. "I'd like to ask a favor of you, though."

His hand was warm and Marge experienced a glow of pleasure. It was lovely walking home with Rod in the soft autumn night—the patches of light and shadow on the uneven sidewalk, the lighted windows in the houses they passed, the distant radio music coming to them through open doors along the familiar streets.

"What's the favor?" she asked, sure in this charmed moment that she would want to do whatever he asked.

"Get a date for Jerry. He won't go unless some girl invites him."

It was ice water dashed against her new happiness. A date for Jerry!

"But . . . who . . . ?" How could she ask anyone to invite Jerry? How could Rod expect her to, after the way Jerry had behaved? "Who?" she repeated and her voice sounded strange and hoarse.

"Couldn't you get Carol to ask him?"

"I'm sure she's going to ask Lewis Tanner, if she hasn't already," she told him.

"What about Lois?"

Marge could scarcely trust her voice. "Rod, you know she's too young for Jerry. He'd turn her down if she did ask him. And besides, her folks wouldn't let her go with a boy two classes ahead of her." They wouldn't let either girl go with Jerry, Marge knew well enough. Why was Rod asking this impossible favor? Didn't he realize . . . Or was she being selfish and mean and small in thinking no one she knew would want to date Jerry?

"Okay. You probably couldn't ask either of the Digbee twins. I guess there isn't anybody." He dropped her hand. "Well, here we are."

They stopped in front of her home.

"Would you like to come in?" Marge asked. She tried to sound cheerful but their moment of understanding was lost. She didn't want him to come in now.

"Some other time," Rod said quietly. "I'd like to get back to *The Clarion* and see what Shorty knows. Give me a rain check?"

She said she would, and sick at heart went up the steps.

It wasn't her fault that Jerry had no friends at school . . . that he had been practically a truant . . . that she couldn't ask any girl she knew to invite him to the Hop.

CHAPTER X

A SIGN COMES DOWN

Marge had not expected to find Bill Tanner at her home when she walked into the living room. Her parents were eagerly listening to his account of what had happened at the citizens' meeting. When she came into the room it seemed to her they all pounced on her at once. She couldn't think any more about Jerry, and whether she had been right or wrong, just then.

"Where have you been?" Janey demanded. "Why didn't you come home with Bill?"

"I looked for you," Bill said accusingly.

"Maybe we shouldn't have done it," Marge began.

" 'We?' " Bill questioned. "You must mean Rod." His tone was so disapproving that Marge was immediately defensive.

"We wanted to know what happened," she said, sitting down firmly in a big living-room chair. Bill wasn't going to scare or silence her now. "We didn't think Mr. Digbee had any right to keep us from knowing, so we slipped backstage and listened for a while."

They all might disapprove, but they wanted to know what she had heard, just the same.

"Suppose everybody had tried that trick?" Dad's frown indicated plainly that he did not condone it.

"We'd all have been caught and sent home, I suppose," Marge admitted.

"Well, what did you hear—since you did it," Janey questioned.

"We couldn't see the pictures but there was a lot of applause at the end," Marge began. "Then the X-Ello people answered questions about what they plan to do if they buy Dodd Park. But Mr. Digbee kept needling them. When we left, Dr. Tozian was trying to get people to think about the future of Eastfield, and he said . . ."

The doorbell interrupted her. It was Mrs. Brundage. She stood in the living room doorway beside Mother who had answered the bell, her thin lips a thinner line than usual in her severe face.

"Dr. Ragland, I'd like to talk to you," she began. He had risen when she came in but she towered a head above him, a formidable woman indeed. "In your study," she added.

Janey was also on her feet. "We have homework so we'll go now," she said and Bill and Marge followed her into the hall. While they said good night Mrs. Brundage opened the alligator bag which seemed part of her every costume. Marge cringed when she saw, jammed in the top, issues of the school paper.

Hurrying upstairs, she could scarcely wait until the door of their room was closed behind herself and Janey.

"Did you see what she had?" Marge whispered. The expression on Janey's face told her well enough that Janey had seen too.

"She's going to influence Dad if she can," Janey said. "Our articles must be getting attention for someone to have brought the school papers to her."

"People are reading them," Marge agreed. "It's about the

most important thing the school paper ever did. All of the kids have been taking their copies home. They've written the articles or are going to, so they want their parents to read them. I've got six more lined up; seven if I can find someone to write on vocational agriculture."

They sat on their two beds and looked at each other across the room. It was the first time in weeks that Marge and Janey had been drawn together. Now they were on the same side of an important question, and opposing them was Mrs. Brundage!

"Do you suppose she can get Dad to stop us?" Marge asked. Janey bit her lip and shook her head.

"He's always supported Superintendent Griffin," Janey said thoughtfully. "Dad's for better schools. How could he take any other position when he's trying so hard to get more money for the college that he can hardly think of anything else? But this X-Ello open forum meeting complicates things."

She looked at her watch. "Let's see if the Andover City station has any news you didn't hear. You weren't there at the end."

Janey snapped the radio on and turned the dials, toning the volume low.

"I feel like the underground," she said in a hushed voice, crowding forward.

"Tonight Eastfield seethes like two armed camps, people either for or against sale of their inherited Dodd Park to the X-Ello company. At the end of a stormy open forum meeting in the old high school auditorium, a resolution was passed calling upon the Board of Aldermen to put the question on the spring ballot. The resolution will be put in proper written form by high school social studies teacher Dr. Aaron Tozian and a committee will get needed signatures. The motion passed over a small but noisy opposition led by Hugh Digbee and a group of vocal aldermen who condemned the entire proceedings as a high-handed attempt to take authority from the properly elected Eastfield officials. A final protest was aimed at Superintendent Griffin for allowing two high school girls to wage a campaign for a costly, modernistic new school building which Eastfield could not afford without the X-Ello sale."

"Oh, no!" Janey gasped and Marge felt as though the green walls of their room were closing in on her. She had unwittingly drawn Janey farther into the battle for the X-Ello sale than her sister had foreseen when the series in the school paper started.

"We didn't expect to get everything we all wanted," she heard Janey saying, more to strengthen her own position than to enlighten Marge.

A tap on their door, a "Yes, come in," from Janey who turned off the radio, and their father entered the room. He drew a chair up between them, crumpling Janey's favorite hooked rug with disregard, and folded his hands tightly between his knees.

"Don't let this broadcast disturb you too much," he said, but he looked serious.

"It does disturb me," Janey said, pushing her hair back off her neck nervously. "I started this series of articles. I told Marge to get the kids to write."

"Whose idea was it in the first place?" Dad asked.

"Mine," Marge admitted, hating to face him.

"Were you the one who proposed having the Chamber of Commerce students attend the meeting?" she heard him ask.

"Nobody expected anything like this," Janey came to her defense. "I don't think Superintendent Griffin thought there would be such a clash. Or that we'd be drawn into it."

Their father looked at the silent radio for a few moments without commenting. Had Superintendent Griffin expected it, Marge wondered. Surely he knew better than the Chamber of Commerce members that all would not be harmonious at the meeting tonight.

"I've been in touch with Superintendent Griffin," Marge heard her father say. "He believes you have a right to express your desires in your school paper. He wrote the factual footnotes on costs, so no one could be misled, or think he didn't have the situation in hand. I'm sure he'll want you to go on with the articles."

He cleared his throat and Marge knew he was not through. He turned his chair slightly in her direction, rumpling the rug once more.

"But Marge, this Chamber of Commerce . . ." Again he paused, the worry lines in his forehead deepening. "I believe young citizens should be informed. Should be prepared to participate in civic affairs. But this X-Ello issue is getting to be dynamite. Before you propose anything more, suppose you take it up with me."

She said "Yes, Dad." She knew she would not dare make another suggestion for the Chamber of Commerce. It was the first important group she had ever belonged to—the group at school which everyone envied and talked about. Mr. Digbee might have been out-voted tonight, but if everyone's father thought as her father did, Mr. Digbee had won against student participation in Eastfield affairs.

School buzzed the next day with varying reports of the forum meeting, but the talk died quickly. Very few thought the ouster of the Chamber of Commerce group from the forum meeting affected their own school paper and no one withdrew from a promise to write. Besides, there was the Harvest Hop to talk about.

"It doesn't make any difference now if there are more boys than girls," Marge told everyone who would listen, hoping the word would get to Jerry and he might come. There might be others without dates she tried to tell herself, but she knew how improbable that was. "We all want to help Mr. Mc-Govern, so everyone should come!"

"But for the Hop in the evening you want a partner," Carol reminded her. "You asked Rod, didn't you?"

"Oh, sure," Marge said in as casual a voice as she could manage, trying not to remember how unhappily the walk home and her invitation had ended. "Are you going with Lewis?"

"My first break-through into the Tanner orbit," Carol said. "What will you wear?"

So they discussed clothes, and who had invited whom, and what they would do if it rained . . . until the important Saturday finally came.

It was only a short walk to the McGovern farm, the first one at the edge of town. Rod had come for Marge and she was pleased that he wasn't dressed in the sophomore's blue-jean uniform. His beige slacks were new and his dark brown shirt had a smart Hollywood styling that she admired. He had never looked so grown up and she was sure her mother approved of his manners as well as his clothes. He was as polite and well-groomed as Bill, who already had started ahead with Janey.

They walked together in groups, mainly by classes, but Marge's hope that this Hop would not be a couple affair was soon dissipated. There weren't any singles and Jerry was nowhere to be seen. They jumped the little ditch at the edge of the highway, raced past the garish sale sign and across the open meadow to the orchard. The rich, tangy freshness of ripened fruit, the spiced odor of apples on the ground, already slightly fermented, was delightful.

Mr. Matthews was there ahead of them with the county agricultural agent, who at once took charge. Somewhat doubt-fully Mr. McGovern watched from the side of his barn.

"We'll work in groups for the afternoon," the county agent shouted, trying to quiet his noisy helpers. "Boys over here to the trees first; girls stay with Mr. McGovern until I can show you how to sort the apples he's already picked."

They scanned the low-growing, crooked trees, gnarled and full-leaved. Splashes of red in the higher branches indicated that Mr. McGovern either had not seen all of his fruit or had not risked getting it.

"There's a knack to picking apples, boys," the official instructed. "You twist the stem slightly without breaking the twig the fruit hangs from. That way you don't damage what we call 'bearing wood.' And don't throw the apples anywhere. Handle them like eggs. Put them in the sacks we have for you and come down the ladders carefully."

Next he instructed the girls in the methods of sorting Extra Fancy, Fancy, and Choice apples.

It was a real workout with the county agent constantly inspecting the baskets. Marge learned how to judge apples by color, size and perfection. She inspected, weighed, and separated into the market baskets until her back ached and the crop was a red blur.

At 3:30 Mrs. McGovern came to the orchard carrying a dishpan heaped with fresh friedcakes. From the coolness of the storage house jugs of cider were brought out. For half an hour after they had eaten, girls and boys stretched out in the shade of the trees to rest.

Marge closed her eyes. Sunlight filtered through leaves crinkled and curled by the first cool nights of fall. In the distance bluebirds and robins sang and on the ground around her, less cowed by the horde of apple pickers, English sparrows twittered. An ant crawled along her arm and an occasional grasshopper chirped beside her. The murmur of voices around her was a pleasant medley, now that the excited shouting had ended.

She wondered where Rod was. Because of his arm he was not allowed to pick, and had been assigned the job of tugging baskets of apples into the barn after the girls had filled them. He had joked with everyone all afternoon, but had found little to say to her. Was he blaming her because Jerry wasn't there?

She felt a tassled grass swish against her nose and opened her eyes to look into his sun-tanned face.

"A penny for your dream," he said. He smiled but his eyes were serious.

"Dreamless sleep," she answered, stretching her arms and trying not to think of Jerry. Was he counting out papers for the newsboys now, more hurt and bitter and resentful than ever? Or had he abandoned Eastfield entirely for the unknown pleasures of Andover? She could scarcely blame him if he had. Should she have tried to pressure somebody into inviting him today? Suppose he never came back to school at all?

The sound of an automobile coming along the meadow road distracted her and she moved her head, trying to see who was coming.

"It's Shorty," Rod told her.

She sat up quickly. "You mean . . . ?" She knew her voice reflected her alarm. She wished, the next moment, that she had not said anything, and tried to look placid.

"He wouldn't have come for me if Jerry hadn't shown, if that's what you're thinking," Rod said almost gruffly. "He'd have counted out himself. He's going to take pictures of our 'Harvest and Hop' for his story."

"I'm sure everything's all right," Marge said. "And pictures of our Hop will be swell."

But Rod was not to be deterred. "Of course, everything's all right," he said. "Jerry told me he'd count out and he will. Next week I take my old job back. He must feel terrible, but he'll do as he promised. Can't you ever forget that once he wasn't able to make it? It wasn't his fault. I know, because I was with him."

He sounded annoyed if not downright angry. This was their first date and the dance was still to come. It mustn't be spoiled! Even if she had been heartless, this date mustn't be spoiled!

"I'm sorry, Rod," she said softly. "But actually, I hadn't mentioned Jerry."

He was subdued by her tone. "I know. Come on and let's get in some of the pictures," he said. He jumped to his feet and took her hand, leading her back to the baskets of apples, gleaming red in the sun.

Shorty took pictures of boys on ladders going up into the apple trees. He took pictures of girls sorting, of the agricultural agent pointing to the market baskets, and Mrs. McGovern passing cider. He was particularly nice to Mr. McGovern and had him pose with Janey, the prettiest girl there.

"I'll come back tonight for a shot or two of the dance," he promised. "So limber up, Mr. McGovern. This is the first barn dance we've had in ages!"

Marge watched the farmer walk with careful steps to Shorty's car. They stood for a long time talking before Shorty drove away.

By six o'clock the McGovern apple orchard was stripped of its Golden Delicious and McIntosh crop. Each variety was separately sorted and graded and ready for crating. Less than perfect fruit was piled in old barrels for the cider mill, and a corps of weary workers was ready for the grilled hamburgers and weenies, the mustard and chili sauce and cole slaw, the potato salad, and the pies and cakes which a committee of mothers had provided. Long tables in the McGovern back yard, close by the open fireplaces were inviting. When the musicians arrived, everyone was ready for the barn dance.

The rough floor of the old barn, which had been used only for the apple crop for years, had been swept and scrubbed for the occasion and Marge wondered whether Mrs. McGovern had done all of the work herself or whether the Hop committee had been busy too. Bouquets of autumn wild flowers filled tin pails and garden sprinkler cans that hung from the rough walls around the room. Cattails and branches of sumac bobbed from old milk cans. Ears of corn hung from the rafters and baskets of apples interspersed benches along the walls. Mr. Matthews and Dr. Tozian pushed the last of them into place.

A violin tuned up, then began to play. Accordion and drum joined in the harmony and boys and girls who had been loitering in the yard hurried to the barn. Mr. McGovern called the first dance.

> "All join hands and round you go . . .
> "Salute your partner, right and left . . ."

Rod smiled at Marge and bowed low. The flickering lantern light gleamed on his dark hair. He linked his arm through hers and swung her lightly around.

The dream she had cherished of her first date with Rod dissolved in the gaiety of the country square dance. It would not have been possible to convert the high school gymnasium into anything so bright and fragrant, so truly a countryside at harvest time, as this festive barn had become. This was more fun than anything she had imagined.

Marge had forgotten about Shorty and his promise to return

for more pictures until he reappeared. Once more he seemed intent upon photographing Mr. McGovern with his young guests. Marge and Rod stood in the open doorway watching while the farmer and a pretty girl went through some of the dance steps. When Shorty put his camera back in its case, Mr. McGovern followed him out of the barn and again they stood talking beside Shorty's car.

The music started up, but Rod did not go back to the dance. Instead he stood in the shadow of the barn, his arm linked in Marge's, watching his uncle. At last they saw Shorty take a paper from his inside coat pocket and give it to Mr. Mc-Govern.

"H-m-m-m-m," Rod said with a knowing nod. "Marge, I've an idea that I've been *had*. That Shorty!"

"What do you mean?" Marge questioned. She didn't understand what Rod's words implied.

Instead of answering, Rod watched Mr. McGovern walk slowly from the car to his house, still holding the paper in his hand.

When Marge and Rod turned to watch the dancers who had continued their fun, they found Dr. Tozian in the doorway. He made no move to leave and they knew he had witnessed the same scene as they, and had heard Rod's remark, too.

"If you were—an unwitting conspirator, shall we say—I think it was in a good cause," the instructor said quietly.

In the white light of a full moon they watched Shorty's car bounce over the rough meadow road, while Marge pondered the conversation between Rod and the instructor. What were they talking about? Near the highway Shorty stopped and walked to the "Lots for Sale" sign. He pulled at the posts that held it up and shoved at the framework with his shoulders. Finally it toppled, face down to earth. Then he got into his car and drove away.

"You mean because we helped with the apples, Mr. Mc-Govern isn't going to sell lots?" Marge asked.

"Something like that," Rod explained. "I don't know what

the deal is yet. I don't know what that paper is that Shorty gave Mr. McGovern, but I'll find out." He hesitated. "This whole idea of the 'Harvest and Hop' was Shorty's," he confided. "He sold me on it, but he sure didn't let me in on everything."

Surprised, Marge weighed the news without replying and Dr. Tozian watched Rod for a moment before he spoke. He didn't seem too surprised.

"It served one good purpose, whatever is behind it," he said. "We don't want a Shacktown here, do we Rod?"

Rod didn't answer. Marge felt his unexpected shudder as he stood beside her, still holding her arm.

CHAPTER XI

SHACKTOWN

MARGE HAD HOPED she wouldn't see Jerry until the Hop was forgotten and the school began to talk about something else. Except for brushing past him in the corridors, she didn't. Rod's arm was out of the sling now and Jerry had given up the paper route as he had promised, so he was no longer at *The Clarion* after school. If he was helping his father, it must have been in the back shop for he never was in sight in the store when Marge passed on her trips to the newspaper office.

Marge wanted to ask Rod about him. She wanted to ask what Rod had learned about the transaction—if there was one—between Mr. McGovern and Shorty on the night of the party, too, but Rod gave her little opportunity. After social studies class he invariably dashed downstairs to the wood-working shop to meet Jerry. After he had delivered his newspapers he did not return to *The Clarion*. At least he had not on the nights when Marge was there reading proof.

It was after Christmas before the X-Ello offer zoomed into the headlines again. Rod burst into social studies class one morning with a commanding "Hear this!"

The rumble of conversation quieted.

"The Board of Aldermen is going to consider the petition to put the X-Ello deal on the spring ballot when they meet next Monday night," he announced. "You must know that," he added looking at Dr. Tozian accusingly.

"Yes," Dr. Tozian admitted. "The committee got enough names on the petition and filed it on time. The aldermen kept it quiet, I guess."

"If it's on the spring ballot, people are sure to vote to sell, aren't they?" Marge asked while everyone crowded nearer Dr. Tozian's desk at the front of the room.

"The sale will have a chance now, shall we say," Dr. Tozian answered. He pressed his hands together with the nervous gesture they knew so well by now.

After class Rod stopped in the hall and waited for Marge.

"Nobody proposed that we go to this meeting, I noticed," he began.

"It was just as well," Marge answered. "Our Chamber of Commerce got Dr. Tozian into enough of a spot the last time we went to an open forum meeting—so called."

Rod nodded in agreement. "I have an idea though," he said moving out of the stream of traffic to lean against the corridor wall. "Why don't we meet at *The Clarion* Monday night? I could have a party. Not much. Potato chips and cokes or something. We'd be there when Shorty gets back from the meeting and we'd know what happened. We could make a report to our classes the next day. I don't see how that could do any harm, do you?"

Marge hesitated. "Just the Chamber of Commerce members?" she asked. "Would the Digbee girls come? I hate to be the only girl."

They considered it. "The Digbee girls wouldn't come, probably," Rod conceded. "I was thinking of inviting some of our friends, anyway. Carol and Lois. Both of the Tanner boys. . . ." He made a wry face when he mentioned them. "Would Janey come?" He hesitated and then added defiantly, "This time we could invite Jerry."

It wasn't right to leave Jerry out of everything and Marge's conscience still pricked. Would Janey come? Carol and Lois? They would be more tolerant than her own sister; they would want to come.

"People should see what he's done in woodworking," Rod went on when she did not immediately reply. "Mr. Matthews says he's going to enter Jerry's breakfront in the Regional Industrial Arts Awards. He's kept after Jerry so his attendance record isn't so bad. He's not an actual truant."

"What about his grades?" Marge asked.

"He ought to squeak through with C's."

Marge drew a long breath. To invite Jerry would not meet with Bill's approval. Probably Janey wouldn't come, for she was busy trying to keep the school clubs going. But Marge could not hedge this time.

"I think you should invite him," she said. "He's your friend and it's your party. I don't know anything about Janey's calendar, but there's no reason why I couldn't come. I'll ask at home."

"I'm glad it's okay with you, for I intended to invite him," Rod said and the set of his chin told her he meant it. "I'll have to clear with Shorty first. It's his office, but he shouldn't say no."

It gave Marge an opening and a change from the subject of Jerry.

"Rod, did you ever find out about Shorty and the sale sign, and the paper he gave Mr. McGovern and everything?"

But already he was edging toward the stairway and the woodworking shop.

"I haven't given up on it," was all he said. "I'll call you about Monday night."

News of Rod's party got around school quickly.

"It's sort of off-beat and really exciting," Carol said, squeezing Marge's arm and surveying every student they passed questioningly, as though deciding whether Rod had included that particular boy or girl. "Everybody has parties in their own homes, but at *The Clarion!* I suppose Rod couldn't have a party where he and Shorty live. I wonder how they do live."

Marge didn't know. A party at *The Clarion* surely was different.

"I was afraid Mom wouldn't let me go," Carol went on breathlessly, falling into line with Marge at the lunchroom. "I told her about the Chamber of Commerce and that you were going and maybe Janey. I didn't mention Jerry. Do you know whether Rod has invited him? He wouldn't, would he? To a party?"

"It's more like a club meeting than a party," Marge explained. "You know why he's having it. And it's only 'maybe Janey.' She said she was pretty busy when Rod called us." She hesitated, drew a quick breath and went on. "As for Jerry, he's invited, Carol, and I'm glad. If we hadn't left him out of everything when he was new and—well, not so friendly and feeling strange—things might have been different."

Carol looked defensive, started to speak then shrugged. "Maybe," she said. "Anyway, we're going to Rod's party."

As it turned out, Janey decided she was too busy to go, but since Marge could go with Carol and Lois, and Dr. Tozian would be there, her father did not object and gave Marge permission to go.

On the night of the party a heavy snow was falling and the air was biting, but lights blazed cheerfully in the front office of *The Clarion* and the building was warm inside. Shorty's long table was covered with a flowered paper table cloth quite out of keeping with the season. Paper plates were heaped with crackers and cheese sticks, potato chips and pickles and olives.

Marge surveyed the room, now so unbusinesslike; such a strange combination of party and office, smelling of food and paste and printers' ink all at the same time. At the far end a door had been opened and from it a radio brought music.

Marge realized she had never seen beyond that door before. She had thought it led to Mr. Whiting's private office and perhaps it did, but first there was a small room with an assortment of radio tubes and equipment, shining black and chrome under a strong, electric bulb hanging uncovered from the ceiling.

Rod's guests soon had typewriter stands pushed back against the wall and were dancing around the long table. Marge stood to one side watching the front entrance where Rod greeted each arrival. Would Jerry come, she wondered.

Bill Tanner swung her into the dance. If Jerry came and asked her to dance, she would, of course. Then the other girls would be polite to him too, and make him one of them at last.

But Jerry did not come. Rod remained in the front office most of the time, watching the door and his laughing guests alternately, until Shorty and Dr. Tozian returned from the meeting. He followed them into the office and turned off the radio while they shook the snow from their overcoats and hats and hung them on the backs of chairs.

The men weren't smiling, and they greeted the revellers with a quiet "Hi." Shorty's thin face twitched nervously from time to time. Dr. Tozian stuffed his hands into his pockets, pulled them out, and wiped his forehead with a wrinkled handkerchief. His black hair wasn't as neat as usual and his tie was twisted to one side. Odd, it seemed.

"I'm glad you didn't ask to attend this meeting and that none of you went," he began. "If you had, it would have been unfortunate, for you might have been unjustly accused."

Rod asked the question that was on everyone's lips: "Accused? Of what?"

"Responsibility for the fist fight that followed," Dr. Tozian told them. "It will be in the paper tomorrow night, but I hope you'll say as little about it as possible in class."

"Fist fight!" It came with gasps of astonishment. "What happened?"

"The aldermen voted to put the question of the sale on the

spring ballot, but the vote was close," he began. "It came after the mayor announced that the School Board is going to ask for a bond issue for a new school. They haven't decided how much money to ask for. Unfortunately they can't wait until after the X-Ello vote is taken or the building program won't get under way in time for you to have a new school next fall."

"Can we report that much?" Marge persisted.

Dr. Tozian nodded. "Now I think you should finish up your refreshments and go home. This is Shorty's office and he has work to do."

They helped Rod clear the table, stack the coke bottles in their containers, and get the office furniture back where it belonged while Dr. Tozian told them sketchily of the actual physical battle that followed the meeting. Someone had accused Dr. Tozian again of "brainwashing" the aldermen at the citizens' open forum meeting. The mayor and some of the aldermen came to his defense, but not until he had actually been knocked down the steps of town hall when the session ended in a noisy word battle.

The Chamber of Commerce members and their friends were speechless. No wonder Dr. Tozian's hair was dishevelled and his tie awry. It was a wonder he was as calm and well-organized as he appeared.

"We'll go right away," Bill Tanner announced. "We'll take the girls home and come back for you. . . ."

Dr. Tozian thanked him. "There won't be a repetition of what happened, I'm sure," he said and Shorty assured Rod and his friends that the troublemakers were the humiliated ones.

The story was in *The Clarion* the next night with more details than Dr. Tozian had revealed at the party. Mr. Digbee had again led the opposition and had started the fight. But he had not kept the X-Ello sale off the ballot. There would be bitter campaigning in Eastfield now.

Janey and Marge read the story together at the end of the afternoon, sitting side by side on the living room davenport.

124

"Do you want to go on with your campaign now?" Janey asked. "I don't think Superintendent Griffin will expect it, if you don't want to. Maybe one campaign in Eastfield is enough."

"I'm not going to quit now unless he says I should," Marge told her sister. "There'll be no plastics course or the things the others want, if we give up now."

Janey seemed relieved. "It's up to you. I don't want our series to stop."

So doggedly Marge went on with her campaign, and supporting her were the rule-box statements by the superintendent. Each new feature would require additional teachers, classrooms, laboratories, money for equipment. The students at Eastfield High School knew what they wanted and their superintendent knew what it would cost the taxpayers.

More than once, as the winter weeks slipped by, Marge wondered whether it would be possible to get Jerry to write the final article about the vocational education department at Andover City High School. He had been happy, and a part of the school, there. Here nothing but the woodworking shop challenged him. Nothing but the breakfront interested him.

When the second semester brought an opportunity for students to select again the out-of-school activities they preferred, she had her chance to talk to him. As usual he was alone, lounging near the stairway and watching the others who crowded around tables in the main hall where they signed up for their favorite activity. As though defying the school's "No smoking" rule, he held an unopened package of cigarets in his hand. Here it was, the beginning of the second semester and Jerome Chamberlin was no more a part of the school than the day he had enrolled.

Carol would question her! Janey might not approve, but Marge pushed her way through the crowd to his side.

"Hi, Jerry. Why don't you sign up for Journalism?" she asked. "Rod belongs. You know more about newspapers now than you did when school started."

He stuffed the package of cigarets into his pocket, the old, appraising look in his eyes.

"It couldn't be that your campaign is running out of ammunition, could it?" he asked. "Even so, me?"

Marge choked back an angry retort. She hadn't invited him for her own purposes entirely. She could ask him to write an article without inviting him to join the Journalism Club.

"So I had an ulterior motive," she said as lightly as she could. "I also thought you might have fun."

"Fun?" he smiled an odd smile. Marge wished she had not made the gesture. She looked at her classmates, pushing and shoving around the tables and was relieved to see Rod coming toward them.

"I guess I just got the brush-off," she told him. "Jerry wants no part of Journalism. Perhaps you can interest him in something else."

"I don't know what it would be," Rod said. "Even the Chamber of Commerce is a washout now. It started out great, but look what happened! Just a re-hash of what we've read in our classroom magazine."

"But you aren't dropping out?" Marge asked in some alarm. "That won't do any good."

Rod and Jerry were both turning away from her. "I'll stay with Journalism," Rod promised. "The Chamber of Commerce?" He shrugged and was off.

There wasn't anything more she could say. She wondered if Rod would spend even more time with Jerry now. There was a definite lessening in club activities. Some of the parent-leaders had found their responsibilities greater than they had expected, or for other reasons had been forced to withdraw. The novelty of the two platoon system had worn off, and the good-will, make-do spirit had been dulled by many minor irritations.

By the time winter snows had melted and the first fresh green of spring had softened the bare branches of shrubs and trees, the students of Eastfield had written of the school they wanted—of everything from jewelry making to rocket research.

"I should have one final wind-up article," Marge told Janey as she took the copy for another edition of the school paper from her sister.

"You may think of something," Janey said. "I'll try to think too. You shouldn't just stop, without an ending. You've done a good job. Everybody says so."

"Who?" Marge asked, tucking the big manila envelope under her arm.

"Bill. Superintendent Griffin. Dad."

"Dad?" Marge asked. "He hasn't said anything to me about it."

"Dad's harassed by important things at the college," Janey excused him. "Politics and things we don't know about. I ask him more questions and talk to him more than you do."

It was true. When Marge thought of her father it was always to vision a worried face and eyes that were seeing something beside herself. When he did concentrate on her, it was because she had made some stupid mistake that had annoyed him. She gave the envelope a tighter squeeze under her arm. Dad thought she had done a good job with her series of articles, and the thought was comforting.

"I'll get lunch before I go to *The Clarion*," she said. "I haven't eaten, have you?"

"At home, in a hurry," Janey told her, so Marge went to the lunchroom alone. She decided to be late in arriving at *The Clarion*. Perhaps Rod would ask her to walk his route with him. It had been weeks since they had done the trip together. All through the winter when the walks had been covered with ice and snow, and bitter winds had howled around street corners, he hadn't asked her. Perhaps he had thought she wouldn't enjoy it and would say no. And most of this spring it had rained steadily. It seemed to Marge she couldn't remember when there had been any sunshine.

She waited until it was time for Rod to start his route. Then she deposited the envelope in the wire basket on Shorty's table and walked through the composing room and the press-room to the alley. Rod had just given the last of the newsboys his count of papers. He stacked his own in his canvas bag and slipped the strap over his shoulder. Then he looked up and saw her watching him.

"Hi! You're late today."

"Yes, I just got here." She hoped he would think something important had kept her.

"Going my way?"

"It's on the way home," she said.

They started up the street together, laughing at little things while Rod put his papers inside each store, never carelessly throwing them across the street. When Marge brought up the subject of how to close her series in the school paper, Rod became serious. They walked the last block of his route in thoughtful silence. Not until an auto horn signalled insistently did either of them see the red convertible at the curb, Jerry at the wheel.

"How about a little ride in the country?" he called. "It's a nice spring day for a change. Stopped raining at last."

Marge tried to hide her surprise and annoyance. Rod had just begun to think about her problem. Why did Jerry have to appear at this moment? Now he would take Rod away from her again. She acknowledged his greeting with a wave of her hand.

"Maybe you'll think of something, Rod," she said. "If you do, let me know." She took a few steps in the direction of Jewett Avenue.

"Come on, Marge," Jerry called to her. "I'm asking you."

Marge slowed her steps to a stop. Would Rod think she was snubbing Jerry if she didn't go? Was Jerry trying to make up for his bruskness when she had made her one gesture of friendliness a few weeks ago? It was mid-afternoon and a ride in the country was appealing. Besides, Rod would be along.

She turned to him questioningly, and in time to see him scowling at Jerry.

Rod, who had been angry when she had not tried to get a date for Jerry for the Hop, who had invited his friend to the party at *The Clarion* and had expected her to welcome him, now didn't want her to go with the two of them for a short ride in the country. Why?

Well, she would go! Perhaps she would find out where Jerry and Rod went almost every afternoon after school. She walked to the car and got in, Rod following her.

It was Jerry who was cheerful and talkative as the car swung along Main Street and out onto Highway Four. Long before they reached Andover, Rod was urging him to turn around.

"We've gone far enough," he said crossly. "Come on, Jerry, let's go back!"

"I thought Marge might like to see you bowl," Jerry said, increasing his speed.

"Well, she wouldn't! And I don't feel like bowling!" Rod was frowning openly, but Jerry drove on. At the outskirts of Andover City he turned from the main highway and followed a cut-off Marge had never explored in her trips with her parents or friends. In another few minutes she knew what Dr. Tozian had meant when he referred to Andover City's Shacktown.

Jerry slowed to twenty miles an hour when he drove through an unpaved street where dogs and chickens and noisy children dodged out of his way, and women carrying brown paper bags of groceries shrugged at his warning horn. There were no sidewalks. The one-storied houses they passed were mostly unpainted, crowded together, with outhouses at the rear of many of the narrow lots. Even the few trees seemed stunted and malformed. A grocery store, drug store, and gasoline station marked the intersection of the two main streets of Shacktown. Beyond the red gasoline pumps, a low cement block building supported a faded blue sign that read *BOWLING*. Between the two buildings, Marge saw a dingy shed with one wide, sagging door swinging and creaking in the wind. Jerry drove into the dim interior and Marge could see two other cars. One was the blue hot-rod she had not seen since the night a stone shocked Eastfield. She sat in her seat motionless, staring at it, and the new safety seat belt that dangled from one side.

"Hop out," Jerry said. When she did not move, he turned to look at her questioningly. "Mine," he went on with the first note of pride she had ever heard in his voice. "Didn't Rod tell you?"

She shook her head, still eyeing the sleek lines of the blue, stripped-down car.

"Well, come on," Jerry said, dismissing it. "We'll show you what it means to roll a strike."

Marge thought there was something almost malicious about his smile as she got out. She looked at Rod and his face was grim.

The ground between the garage and bowling alley was bare of grass, unpaved and uneven. What a forlorn place this was. Why had Jerry brought her here? Not just to let her know he had a hot-rod, she was sure. Why did Rod come? Did Jerry let him drive the racer, or was it because bowling was cheap, and he had so little money to spend. Did Shorty know about this place? The car? The races? And what about the expensive red convertible Jerry sometimes drove? Whose car was it?

The questions crowded into her mind as she followed Jerry out of the garage. No wonder Rod had not wanted Jerry to bring her to this slum. Now they were at his mercy.

"One game," Rod almost growled. "One game and that's it!"

Marge stepped inside the bowling alley and looked around her. Boys and girls her own age or perhaps a few years older, lounged on backless benches along the wall on either side of the door. Two unshaded light bulbs hung from the ceiling over each bowling lane, one at the start and the other over the pins at the finish, about sixty feet away at the far end of the bowling alley. Cigaret smoke filled the air, curling about the glaring overhead lights, and the scent of chalk dust reminded her oddly of school.

There had been a noisy bedlam of talk when they came in, but the raucous laughter subsided at the sight of a stranger. The girls, nearly all dressed in bluejeans and tight fitting sweaters, eyed Marge in her conventional school clothes suspiciously.

"Hi, Champ," a few boys greeted Rod and others looked at Jerry with an occasional sly wink or grin.

"Rod's girl wants to see him make a strike," Jerry explained. "Move along. You don't need the whole bench."

The boy next to the door got up, making room for Marge. Cheeks burning, her indignation mounting, she sat down next to a girl who blew a heavy smoke ring into the air, then moved away without speaking.

Rod's girl! Did they think Rod was going to bring her here again, or that she had wanted to come? She felt as unfriendly as these boys and girls appeared, but there was an inward glow of pleasure at the thought that once more Jerry had called her Rod's girl.

Jerry lounged against the wall beside her while Rod selected a ball. Marge saw him weigh it in his left hand, take a starting position with feet together and shoulders erect, transfer the ball to his right hand. Three quick steps and straight down the alley it went.

"That's the old Champ!" one or two chorused as the pins crashed, one by one.

Marge did not know the rules. She didn't know how many times Rod must knock those pins over before the one game he had said he would play, was over. She waited, miserably, listening to the resounding roll of the ball upon the polished wood of the lane, the final crash.

Suddenly the door beside her opened, then slammed shut immediately and noisily.

"Okay everybody! This is it!" It was a man's voice, severe and harsh. Marge looked into the stern faces of two State

Police officers. What could this mean? Was somebody being arrested? The lights, the shining lanes, the strange faces in clouds of tobacco smoke swam before her eyes.

Marge had not been aware of the manager of the bowling alley until he appeared now, confronting the officers. He was fat and middle-aged, his brown trousers wrinkled and his white shirt soiled and frayed at the neck. He looked mild and good natured.

"Okay, go right ahead," he said. "You've never found anything on my place and you never will. I've told these kids if they ever bring a bottle in here, they'll never come again."

The officers nodded and motioned the lounging boys and girls to one side of the room. They obeyed, with a few insolent remarks. Jerry and Marge moved to a place at the end of the line. While one man watched, the other went methodically around the building, looking under everything. A few sweaters and jackets hung on nails along the whitewashed walls, and these were searched with quick, deft handling.

"Satisfied?" the manager asked. There was an indifferent sneer in his voice, and the young bowlers began muttering among themselves. The door had scarcely closed when their voices rose to a bedlam of abuse.

"Pipe down! Shedup!" the manager shouted. "Play, if that's what you came for."

Marge's heart began to beat normally again. She looked toward Rod who was still standing at the foul line holding a ball in his two hands and glaring at Jerry. Once more the door opened and another voice sounded behind her—a southern drawl which she instantly recognized, only now Morris was singing no love song.

"Jerry, you fool! Where have you been?" Morris asked.

"Here, waiting until the cops were satisfied and left," Jerry answered indifferently. "I got wind they might show up, so I . . . There's nothing to worry about."

"What about the business?"

"Nothing to worry about," Jerry repeated. "I'll get it after

I take this VIP back to Eastfield. I just wanted her to see how the other half live."

Marge heard Morris catch his breath. He hadn't seen her until then and his tone changed at once.

"Miss Ragland! This Jerry character brought you here?" He turned away from her to confront Jerry.

"You know what you should be doing now. Take the car and get to Andover, if you ever want to use it again!" he ordered.

Without a word Jerry slipped out of the door and the next second Morris was beside Marge, on the rough wooden bench.

"I apologize for Jerry," he said in his softest voice. "The idea that he should bring you here! I'll take you home myself, and right away. Maybe you're hungry, I am. There's a swell roadhouse near here . . . good steak dinners . . . It won't be crowded now."

Marge felt her throat grow tight. Jerry had played a contemptible trick on her, but Jerry was the one who had a car, and now Morris had ordered him back to Andover for "the business," whatever that was. She gripped the little billfold she carried and watched her knuckles grow white.

Then she sensed she was not sitting alone with Morris. Rod was standing in front of them, feet apart and the bowling ball gripped menacingly in his two hands.

CHAPTER XII

DARKENING SKIES

In his tight fitting bluejeans and T-shirt, Rod looked not only smaller but years younger than the suave, well-dressed Morris. But the set of his jaw was determined and his stance belligerent.

"I'm taking Marge home myself, Morris," he announced.

In the harsh light of the bleak bowling alley, Marge warmed to his words and his staunch defense of her.

Morris scarcely looked at Rod but smiled ingratiatingly at Marge. "How are you taking her home?" he asked. "She didn't come on an inter-city bus and she's not going home that way. She deserves better."

"I'm taking her home, hear?" Rod repeated, his voice thick with anger.

Marge started to get up, but Morris put a strong hand on her arm and held her back. She was about to jerk herself free when the manager walked over to them.

"Better take your girl and get going, kid," he said quietly to

Rod. "Come back to your job later. How are you fixed for bus fare?"

"Okay," Rod said and walked back to the lane to replace the shining ball. Already the boys and girls had resumed their fun and the sound of crashing pins filled the room.

"Stick around, Morris," the manager said, dismissing both Rod and Marge. "I'd like to be let in on a few things."

Free to leave, Rod took his jacket from the bench where he had thrown it when he came in and led Marge out of the bowling alley.

"It's half a mile to the bus stop," he told her. "I guess we have to walk."

"I'd rather walk all the way home than ever ride with Jerry again," Marge said. "Or Morris either." Involuntarily she shuddered and almost looked back to be sure neither one was following her.

Rod put on his jacket. "I don't blame you," he said. Then he changed the subject. "It's going to rain again."

Marge turned up the collar of her own jacket against the drops that had begun to fall. "I don't mind," she said. "Only now will you tell me why you've been friends with Jerry all year?"

"Yes, I'll tell you," Rod said. "It was Jerry who taught me to bowl. He had the job of pin boy here when I first met him almost two years ago. Shorty had to come out one night to cover a story and he took me along instead of leaving me home alone. He parked me in the bowling alley where I'd have something to do while I waited for him. Jerry was the only one who was decent to me that night. The kids out here don't take to strangers and he wasn't really one of them any more than I was. The Chamberlins didn't live in Shacktown when they were in Andover. They're a good family."

He paused, and Marge waited for him to go on with his story.

"Jerry's dad is pretty gruff with him sometimes. I was surprised that he let you know about his hot-rod. His dad has told him to get rid of it and doesn't know he kept it and races with it."

"How did he get the money for it?" Marge asked.

"Odd jobs. Used some of the money he had in the bank. . . . You must know about the races, Marge. That gets into the papers once in awhile."

Marge tried to remember what she had read. There was nothing wrong with the races. The State Police supervised them. Then she remembered. "Betting?" she asked, and Rod nodded.

"Then there's Morris and 'the business,'" she said in disgust. "What's that? What was Morris growling about? What did he send Jerry to Andover City for?"

Rod didn't answer. They had almost reached the highway and he looked back for the bus.

"We're really going to get wet if it doesn't come along soon," he said. Marge fumbled in her pocket for her plastic rain cap. The sky was completely overcast now. This wasn't going to be a spring thunder shower, but another long, steady downpour.

"You haven't told me about the job Jerry has now," she reminded him.

"Wait," was his only reply, "here it comes." He signalled for the bus to stop and helped Marge up the high steps and into the dry security of the long rows of gray tweed-covered seats. There weren't many passengers and they had no trouble locating two empty seats together.

"Well?" she asked after they had settled down. "You might as well tell me the rest."

Rod fussed nervously with the damp jacket he had draped across his knees.

"You won't tell?" he finally asked. "I've offered over and over to give up this bowling job if he'd take it back. But working for Morris he gets the car to drive and makes more money to spend on his hot-rod. Morris has a lot of connections and sometimes Jerry can get auto parts he needs cheaper through

Morris. Only he'll get caught one of these days and then he'll be in real trouble. I don't know what Shorty'd do if he knew!"

Marge waited and at last he blurted out the truth.

"Jerry's selling beer for Morris. In the garage. He keeps it in the trunk of that broken down car. Morris has more than one kid doing it . . . in dumps like this . . . Beantown . . . You probably never heard of the place. Morris only pays for one license and that's for Andover City, but he sells all around. . . . The manager of the bowling alley here won't have anything illegal on his place, but this old garage isn't his and nobody seems to care what goes on there." He drew a long breath, as though relieved to have confided in her.

"That day when we didn't get back in time for the paper route was another time when the State Police tried to find out who was bringing beer into Shacktown," he went on. "Some kid's folks are always complaining. Jerry had just driven in, and they made him open up the car. There it was, but he hadn't sold one can and he had his story. 'The car belongs to Morris who has a store in Andover and a license to sell there. I didn't know Morris had any beer in the car.' They couldn't prove a thing so they let him go, but they held him until they could check on his story and locate Morris in Andover. He said it was all true. Said he thought it was the next day that Jerry wanted to borrow the car."

Marge stared out of the rain-drenched window, feeling a little sick and wishing she didn't know.

"Aren't you almost a part of it?" she asked, lowering her voice.

"Almost," he admitted. "Jerry drives me out and dumps me at the bowling alley, then he goes into Andover for the beer. I bowl and set up pins and help the manager with the place until Jerry's sold the stuff and loaded up the empties. There isn't an empty bottle or can around when he leaves. The kids watch the road for him. So I tell myself I'm not part of it . . . that if I let Jerry down, all he'd have is Morris and this crummy place. Jerry's got some good, solid stuff, Marge. Look at the way he's always stood by me, when none of my friends would have anything to do with him. But I don't know what Shorty'd do if he found out."

Marge winced. She was one of those who hadn't wanted to have anything to do with Jerry. But she was Rod's friend— hadn't he just said it? She would share his secret and help him if she could.

"I don't know what my folks will do if they find out I've been to that place, to say nothing of this job Jerry has with Morris," she said quietly.

"Do you have to tell them?" Rod asked. "About what Jerry's doing, I mean? If you must tell them about the dirty trick he played when they ask you where you've been, don't let them think I had anything to do with it. You know I didn't, don't you?"

"I know you didn't."

For a time they rode in silence, listening to the swish of the windshield wiper against the rain-drenched glass.

"What are you going to do?" Marge finally asked.

"I don't know," Rod admitted. "If there was only more to do in Eastfield. Ways for a kid to earn a little money and have a little fun. What's Jerry going to do if he gives up this job he does for Morris? That's what he always asks me. He'll have no money to keep his hot-rod going, no car to drive. Mr. Chamberlin's business isn't good enough for Jerry honestly to earn anything at the store and he hates to take money for nothing. Especially to spend it on the hot-rod, which would make his dad madder than ever if he knew Jerry still has it."

Again there was silence. Marge didn't know what to say. Then Rod went on.

"He's really had a rough time, Marge. Having to move here when he didn't want to. The kids didn't try very hard to get him to go out for football. He didn't get elected to the Chamber of Commerce or anything else. Sometimes I wonder what he'll do if things don't change at school next year."

138

"Things aren't likely to change at school unless he changes," Marge said.

Glumly Rod agreed.

"Rod, maybe I shouldn't ask this and don't tell me if you don't want to," Marge said, "but was it Jerry who threw the stone through the town hall window that night?"

Rod looked miserable. She knew he wished she had not asked the question.

"If it wasn't Jerry it was one of the boys with him," Rod admitted. "He was showing off all right, taking out some of his spite against Eastfield. I never asked him and he never told me, but I saw two boys dash into the blue car and he was one of them. He let the other fellows take his car back to Shacktown so he'd be home when his dad came."

"I guess it doesn't matter now," Marge said. "So much has happened since then."

"And none of it good," Rod agreed. "Like this weather. Maybe the bus driver will let you off at your own corner, even though it isn't a regular stop. I'll ask."

He got up and swayed to the front of the bus, spoke to the driver, then signalled for Marge. They stood holding to the hand rail until the bus stopped at Jewett Avenue.

"Don't you get off here," Marge said. "You can dash to *The Clarion* from the bus depot and not get too wet. Only how are you going to get back out there to work tonight?"

"I won't," Rod admitted. "There won't be much doing on a night like this."

He was looking at her intently and she knew what was on his mind. She hadn't promised to keep his secret. The bus drew to a halt and he turned up the collar of her coat while she waited for the driver to open the door.

"I won't say anything tonight," she whispered. "I don't know what we're going to do, but . . ."

He managed a grateful grin. "We'll think of something," he said.

Marge raced along her home street, keeping under the protecting branches of the trees as much as she could. She would have to keep Rod's story confidential, she told herself. He had defended her against Morris, shared his secret with her and no one else. She felt a glow of happiness in remembering the touch of his hand when he turned up her coat collar. Already she shared his desire to help Jerry too.

She couldn't imagine what her father would say if he knew what had happened this afternoon. What would he do if he knew of Jerry's activities? Turn him over to the officers? Marge shuddered at the thought. No, for now at least she could not tell him.

She found the house in such a turmoil when she reached home that she was scarcely questioned. Dad had unexpected guests and from the study came the sound of men's voices in serious discussion. Janey was on the telephone trying to locate someone to help with serving and dish-washing. Mother was in the kitchen.

"Marge, where have you been?" her mother called. "Get out of that wet coat and set the table. For eight."

Janey dialed another number. "Where have you been?" she asked.

Marge skipped upstairs without answering, removed her wet clothes and hastened to set the table. Then there were jars of pickles and jelly to open, salad greens to stretch to serve eight, and too much concern over preparing an adequate dinner without adequate notice for anyone to press Marge for an account of her afternoon activities.

The next day in social studies class Marge was conscious more than once of Rod's questioning eyes. He waited for her after class, and together they walked slowly downstairs to the main corridor.

"They didn't ask me anything at home," Marge said quietly. "There was too much confusion for anyone to think about me."

"Good," Rod answered. "I wouldn't want you to say anything that wasn't true, of course, but . . ." He shook his head dubiously.

"I haven't figured out what we should do," Marge admitted. "How am I to act when I see Jerry?"

"You can't act as though you liked it," Rod conceded. "I'm not going to laugh it off either. There was no excuse for his taking out his spite on you. I'm not going to woodworking to look him up today. He can look me up, for a change."

Rod shifted his books from one arm to another. "I don't make enough money out there to pay, if I have to spend bus fare both ways," he told Marge. "Maybe if I gave up the job he'd take it back and quit selling beer. Only he likes that car . . ."

He left the sentence unfinished and together they stood near the head of the stairs leading to the woodworking shop. They didn't want to see Jerry, yet some force seemed to hold them there. The boys were coming up now, followed by Mr. Matthews. The instructor went to Rod and Marge at once.

"Hello, there. Rod, where's Jerry?"

"Jerry?" Rod repeated. "Wasn't he in class?"

"No, and this time it's serious," Mr. Matthews said. "Last night the judging committee selected Jerry's breakfront as our entry in the Regional Industrial Arts Awards, and today no Jerry!"

Rod whistled softly. "I'll call his father," he offered. "Boy, for him not to show at a time like this!"

"I've already called Mr. Chamberlin," Mr. Matthews said. "Jerry didn't come home last night."

"What?" Both Marge and Rod gasped the word.

"I think his father has an idea where he was. He said he'd look him up as soon as he could close the store this afternoon if Jerry wasn't home by then," Mr. Matthews said.

"What are you going to do? About the Industrial Arts Awards, I mean," Rod asked.

"I'm going to enter his work," the instructor answered. "As

a matter of fact, the boys crated it in class this morning and I'm shipping it this afternoon. But if he doesn't get back in school . . ."

He didn't need to say anything more. If Jerry was suspended for truancy, the Regional Industrial Arts Awards jury would surely disqualify the entry.

"Maybe I could keep the radio shop open for Mr. Chamberlin this afternoon so he could hunt Jerry up," Rod suggested.

"Why don't you offer?" Mr. Matthews asked. "If you have any influence, get him back in school before it's too late."

Marge and Rod watched him walk slowly down the hall toward the superintendent's office.

"Meeting Janey for lunch?" she heard Rod ask dully.

"For the copy anyway," she told him. "Shall we go to the lunchroom now? She'll look for me there."

Lunch was a dismal affair and they started down the rain-drenched street for the newspaper office as soon as they had finished their sandwiches. Water was running even with the curb in some places and at corners they had to leap across streams that the draining system couldn't carry off. When they reached Mr. Chamberlin's store it was closed.

At the newspaper office Shorty was tense and almost curt. For once his smooth hair hung over his forehead, his neatly pressed coat lay carelessly crumpled over his chair.

"If you kids are going to hang around here, make yourselves useful," he said. "You both can read proof. I had to let the proofreader go home and move to higher ground!"

He shoved a long galley proof toward Rod, and they both sat down to read it.

"Flood Threatens Eastfield" was the key.

"We get this every spring," was Rod's comment. "We practically had to swim from school to the office just now."

"We don't get it like this," Shorty said. "Haven't you heard the radio today?"

Marge read the lead story while she waited for Shorty to bring her any other work she could do.

The river was over its banks, flooding Dodd Park.

The State Police were urging people in low-lying areas to evacuate at once.

The weather bureau predicted more rain during the night —no relief in sight.

The telephone jangled and Shorty answered it. "Maguire speaking . . . Yes . . . Yes. . . ." He scribbled in sprawling handwriting on one of the sheets of newsprint that littered the table.

"Boil all water," he repeated. "Emergency clinic at town hall . . ." He handed the notes to Marge. "Type it up," he directed. "All I need is four sentences. Mark it '12 point bold, rule box, single column.'"

Marge did as he told her, then took the copy to the linotype room while Shorty once more answered the telephone. Men there were working at jet speed. She moved out of their way and looked around her. Suddenly her eye caught the protruding drawer of the battered case of shallow shelving.

The type she saw was from the pages of her own school paper—one of her "School We Want" articles. Surreptitiously she opened other drawers. Shorty had saved the type from every article. He had never done that before, she was sure. Why had he saved the type for that controversial series?

CHAPTER XIII

FLOODTIDE

Marge wanted to ask Shorty why he had kept her type, but now was not the time. The telephone was ringing, and from the small room leading to Judson Whiting's private office the radio blared and signal beeps sounded which Marge did not understand.

"Shorty's a ham," Rod explained. "That's his shack and his rig. He built it himself. I know it looks like a moonshiner's still, but he's contacted the South Pole and Hawaii with it. He'll be at it all night, for he can pick up the State Police and pass on whatever instructions they give. They're patrolling the river now, trying to get people to evacuate."

"What are you going to do?" Marge asked.

"Answer the telephone probably," Rod said. "Shorty's taught me the Morse Code and I can do ten words a minute, but he won't let me handle the rig tonight."

They watched while Shorty walked from the phone to his radio equipment. The Andover City station announced that flood instructions would be broadcast every half hour and oftener if necessary.

"Marge, you'd better get home," Shorty called to her. "You can't tramp the route with Rod in this rain, and besides there's going to be work for everybody by morning. Tell your mother to keep the radio on. If telephone lines go down, it's the only communication we'll have. I hope we don't get a power shutdown too."

Marge put on her rain hat and buttoned her coat tightly. Head down against the wind and lashing storm, she made her way up Main Street. Many stores had closed early, and the sky was dark as twilight although it was only mid-afternoon. Branches of trees along Jewett Avenue swayed and bent low. No one was on the street, and the few automobiles were crawling, headlights barely pushing through the gray mist.

At home Mother had the radio on and she and Janey and the Brundage maid were busy rolling bandages.

"I'm glad you're home," Mother said. "You can help too. Try to make some beef stew from the left-over roast for an early dinner. Dad just called and said he wasn't going to get home tonight. The senators who were here last night convinced him he should be at the Capitol today, and now . . ."

The telephone interrupted her and she put her work aside to answer it.

"Yes . . . yes, Mayor, we're already making bandages. . . . Yes, I've alerted all members of the Red Cross. Each member always calls five other members and in no time we have the whole chapter working. We're waiting now for instructions."

She turned from the telephone to the girls.

"The Mayor's issued an emergency order and Superintendent Griffin has opened the school lunchroom and gymnasium for women and children evacuees. Two of the churches will take care of men who aren't able to help with flood relief. I'll marshal bedding and order food right away." She paused and surveyed the room. "Janey, you report to the emergency clinic at town hall as soon as you've had a bite. You've taken first aid, so do the shift up to midnight. I'll have relief for you then and somebody to bring you home."

"What am I to do?" Marge asked.

"Gather up the bedding I'd put away for the summer." She turned to the Brundage maid. "Go see how much bedding Mrs. Brundage can let us have. See if she'll let you stay with Marge tonight."

Mother at once began assigning tasks to the Red Cross members. She scheduled workers and arranged shifts for school and the emergency clinic. As chairman of the local Red Cross, she was prepared and organized.

Marge snapped on the kitchen radio to listen while she put together a quick dinner.

". . . Dodd Park completely inundated . . ."

"Farms in river bend between Eastfield and Andover City in greatest danger. All residents urged to evacuate at once. . . ."

"That means Mr. McGovern," Marge called to her sister who was packing the first aid materials. "I wonder if they have their radio on."

"Hush!"

The announcer went on with emergency instructions.

". . . People in the flood area: If you do not have friends living on high land go to Eastfield High School. Take all the canned food and bedding you can carry. I repeat: Everyone boil all water . . ."

The Brundage maid returned with two laundry bags filled with bedding and Marge brought from the cedar closet the blankets which had been cleaned and put away. It was cold enough to need blankets, even in a dry house high on Jewett Avenue.

"Back out the station wagon, Marge," her mother directed. "It's fortunate you took driver education and have your student license. We'll stop at the police station and get an emergency permit for you, so you can help with the car when we need you."

Marge took Mother to the school first, then Janey to the town hall, driving with extra care although there was almost

146

no traffic. She wanted to stop at *The Clarion* where lights burned in the front office windows and glowed through from the room beyond, but there was no excuse. Cautiously she crawled uphill along deserted Main Street to Jewett Avenue and home. The Brundage maid had not returned and the house was empty and damp. She put paper and charcoal and a few logs on the fireplace and soon had a blaze started. Then she turned on the radio. Perhaps she'd better not undress tonight. She'd get an afghan and curl up on the davenport.

The telephone rang. It was Dad wanting to know where everyone was, and giving his hotel location in the Capitol. He'd be home tomorrow if the bridge between Andover and Eastfield didn't wash out.

Then emptiness and the strange quiet of the house with only the lashing branches outside, and rain pounding against the windows, and the radio to divert her. Marge wished the Brundage maid would come, and was glad when she finally arrived.

She closed her eyes that night with the swish of wind and rain beating through her consciousness. In the morning she woke with an ominous feeling that something was wrong. Where was she? Why was the radio on? Then she remembered and, wide awake, listened to the alarming newscast. There was no let-up in sight. Flood waters had spread over farmlands and orchards and meadows beyond the big bend in the river, during the night. Andover City Red Cross was standing by, and the state agency had underwritten the cost of necessary food and medicine. State Police from three adjacent posts were helping with rescue work. Families who had not heeded yesterday's warning now were marooned.

Marge tossed the afghan aside and tiptoed upstairs. Janey had come in without wakening her and had gone to bed. The Brundage maid was still asleep and Mother had not come home.

Marge fixed a hasty breakfast, then got the station wagon and drove to school. Mother must be dead tired by now.

It was only a little after seven, but from the lunchroom came the stimulating aroma of freshly made coffee and oatmeal cooking. And down the corridors of Eastfield High School a strange assortment of animals sniffed and prowled and occasionally growled and hissed at each other. The evacuees had brought their pets and the first signs of life and smells of food had roused cats and kittens, dogs and puppies, even before weary women and children were up and hunting for the washrooms. Marge stopped for a moment at the entrance to the gymnasium where people still lay on the floor, wrapped in mounds of bedding. There were even bird cages hanging from the basketball net, out of reach of cats. Suitcases and bundles were piled everywhere.

She found her mother in the kitchen.

"You must be dead," she said. "Who's going to relieve you, and when?"

"Oh, we're not so tired," Mother said, but she looked hollow-eyed. Her shoulders seemed to sag under the dark green sweater she had draped around her. "There were two cots in the Ladies' Lounge and a davenport in the Men's Lounge, so we took turns sleeping. But these animals! We hadn't thought of them. Go to the office and call all three grocery stores. See how soon they can get dog and cat food here. If they can't deliver you go get it before the hubbub drives me out of my mind!"

Marge started down the hall, now alive with animals demanding attention.

"Mommy, where are you?" came a wail from the gymnasium.

"I want a drink of water!"

"I'm hungry! I want my breakfast!"

Marge surveyed the half-dressed women and children, the dogs and cats, and shut the door of Superintendent Griffin's office against them while she phoned.

Yes, the grocers had pet supplies and would bring a stock with the first food delivery, but tell Mrs. Ragland the dairy had not gotten in with milk yet. Better start rationing the canned milk right away.

From the superintendent's office Marge went downstairs

where the sound of rhythmic hammering and radio music came from the woodshop. What could be going on there? She peered through the open door. Piles of heavy planks lay on the floor and Mr. Matthews and two of the older boys were busy with saws and spikes and hammers. The instructor scarcely looked up from his work to greet her.

"What have you been detailed to do?" he asked.

"Nothing right now," she told him. "I heard the hammering and wondered what was going on."

"Rafts," Mr. Matthews told her. "The State Police are hampered in their rescue work because people who own boats locked them in their boat houses at the lake last fall and the bridge between Eastfield and the lake is out. No one can get the boats to us."

"How many rafts have you made?" Marge asked. "Can you make enough?"

"We need workers all right," Mr. Matthews admitted. "I've told the mayor. Did Rod find Jerry? He's the best worker I have and I sure need him now."

Rod hadn't seen Jerry last night, she was sure.

"I can call Mr. Chamberlin," she offered.

Mr. Matthews shook his head. "Mr. Chamberlin took his truck and started for the dairy an hour ago. Mayor's orders," he explained. "You haven't got your father's station wagon here, by any lucky chance?"

"Yes, it's here."

"Then if you haven't any other job assigned, would you deliver this raft to the State Police? I hate to let anyone else take the time to do it. Stop at *The Clarion* and see where they want it. Near the McGovern farm, the last word I had. And don't drive off the road. The ground is a quagmire everywhere."

The assignment would give Marge a chance to see Rod and find out what he and Shorty knew. Perhaps Rod had some word from Jerry. If Mr. Chamberlin had located his son last night, it was obvious he had not persuaded Jerry to come home.

The front door of *The Clarion* was unlocked. Marge went in and through the half door to Shorty's city room. The man lay stretched out asleep on one of his long tables, half covered by his rain coat. Coffee stained paper cups littered the table opposite. A half-eaten hamburger bun, smeared with ketchup, told of his latest meal. In "the shack" Rod pawed over dials and knobs and tubes, ear phones over his touseled head. He didn't see or hear her until she touched his shoulder.

"Marge! What are you doing here?" He whispered the words and looked toward Shorty.

"I'm delivering a raft to the State Police somewhere," she told him. "Shorty's to make contact and find out where I'm to go."

"Let Shorty sleep," Rod said and with a switch of the dials he gave his call letters. In seconds he had instructions for Marge. They were to go as near the McGovern farm as she could get. The officers would be on the look-out for her.

Marge started toward the door, then hesitated. "Rod, do you know where Jerry is?" she asked. "Mr. Matthews needs him."

"At the bowling alley, unless he's skipped out," Rod said without looking at her. "He's threatened it. He might figure this is the time with the State Police too busy to check on missing automobiles."

For a moment the full significance of his answer did not come to her. When it did, she was too shocked to reply. Rod was saying Jerry might take the red car and disappear. Take it? Steal it, that was what Rod was really saying.

Marge closed the door of the newspaper office and drove cautiously toward the McGovern farm, her mind once more on Jerry. Here was his chance to prove his real worth—to let Eastfield see the Jerry that Rod knew. Where was he now? What had he done since he embarrassed her so miserably yesterday?

But Marge could not dwell long on Jerry. From the highway she could see the water-covered fields and beyond the bend in the road, the full menace of the disaster.

The swirling, raging river was alive! Henhouses with drenched chickens on the roofs bounced past, swaying and jarring as the precarious perches hit overturned farm machines or stumps hidden by the muddy water.

Horses and cattle floundered against the flood, trying to reach shallow water and dry ground, but all too often carried on with the current in mid-stream.

Dead bodies of birds and cats swirled around in the circling eddies near shore, and bounded on the downstream waves.

An overturned outhouse, on which a shivering dog whimpered, apparently afraid to try its strength against the forces of the water, bobbed and bounced past. Seeing the station wagon the animal wailed mournfully, got up on three feet, then sunk back. One leg trailed over the side of the building. He couldn't swim with a broken leg.

The ominous roar of rushing water rang in Marge's ears, and from the stagnant inlets at the edge of the flood came the stench of farm manure. She slowed the car almost to a stop to watch the destruction. Saplings and branches of larger trees bounded on the tortured brown billows. She had seen storms on the lake, but never anything so vicious as this flood. Nothing but the sturdiest rafts and men of giant strength could keep a straight course in that melee of tossing branches and buildings and floating logs and debris, all forced headlong by the might of the water.

She thought of the McGoverns. Where were they? The river would be billowing above the first floor of their home now, if the house still clung to its foundation. She must hurry to her rendezvous with the State Police. Soon she saw the house, and from the second story window a white pillow case waved in the chill wind. Was this a signal that they had not evacuated and were waiting for rescue? Like others, they probably could not believe the river would swell out more than a mile inland to inundate their orchard and imperil their lives.

The officers were waiting and unloaded the raft quickly.

"The McGoverns?" she asked.

"We're going for them now," one of the men told her. He surveyed the raft. "Tell Mr. Matthews to make the next ones three planks wider," he said.

Marge peered through the rain toward the McGovern house. She thought she could see the aged couple in the window of the second story where the white banner signalled. She strained her eyes. Was it her imagination? But she couldn't sit there and wait. Quickly she started the engine. She should get back to Mr. Matthews who was building more rafts and needed more help.

She should have turned around, but instead she went straight ahead. It would be an hour before Mr. Matthews could possibly have another raft built. Maybe longer, she didn't know. In an hour she could drive to Shacktown and back, easily.

Marge drove as fast as she dared on the rain-drenched road, peering through the blurred windshield for washouts or over-turned trees. The bridge between Andover and Eastfield still held. Turning off at the Shacktown road, she slackened her speed, for the ruts were deep here and no one had cleared rubble or branches away. No one was out in the storm. She drove into the miserable garage with its sagging door, her heart pounding.

The red convertible was there!

So Jerry must be there too. She jumped from the station wagon, crossed the muddy, uneven lot and pushed the door of the bowling alley open. It took all her strength to close it against the wind.

Only a night light at the far end of one lane was burning, and at first Marge thought there was no one in the building. Empty, it seemed longer and more dreary than she remembered it, with its odor of varnish and chalk and stale tobacco smoke. Then from the bench beside her came the scrape of a shoe against the plank floor and Jerry tossed a coat from his shoulders and sat up. It was a moment before either one spoke.

"What are you doing here?" he demanded.

"I came for you." Her voice sounded strange, even to herself.

He stared at her in the dim light. "Why?"

"Because we need you. Mr. Matthews needs you."

"Humph! Like a hole in the head anyone needs me!" He rubbed a shoulder against the rough, unplastered wall and avoided looking at her.

"That's where you've been all wrong from the start," Marge told him. "Eastfield needed you on the football team last fall, but you wouldn't play. We need you to represent us in the Industrial Arts Awards, but where were you for the judging? None of that matters now, though. We need you to help Mr. Matthews build rafts and save lives, Jerry! I've just delivered the first one he made, but he's got to build more. All day today. Maybe all night too. You've got to come back and help."

"I don't see why."

"Because you've got something important to give Eastfield. Maybe you think you don't need Eastfield. Maybe you think selling beer in a broken down garage is fine business, because you get a smart red car to drive. But I don't think you really do. And now's the time to make up your mind."

He got to his feet slowly. "Who sent you here to tell me to make up my mind?"

"Nobody," Marge shot back. "Rod couldn't come because he and Shorty are practically alone at the paper. They worked all night to man the radio that keeps us informed. What we need is rafts. Mr. Matthews said you were the best worker he has. There was nobody to come for you but me."

He pulled the little comb from his pocket and slicked back his hair.

"Miss VIP in Shacktown again! Does the president of the college know you're here?"

Dad! The day of reckoning would come . . . the day when she would have to tell him how involved both she and Rod were with Jerry. He didn't sound as belligerent as at first. She looked at him and the sneer had disappeared from his face. Was he thinking of what she had said instead of feeling sorry for himself?

"No, my father doesn't know where I am or that I've ever been here," Marge said. "Shorty doesn't know what you've been doing, either. When they know, Rod and I have some explaining to do. It will be easier if you're back where you should be, working with the rest of us."

He reached for his coat slowly. Was he coming with her, or leaving in the red car, for where?

"You're really twisting my arm now," he said without looking at her. "But gallant, that's me. Let me open the door for you."

CHAPTER XIV

A CAMPAIGN LOST

"Do you want to drive?" Marge asked when they reached the station wagon in the damp, wind-swept garage. Jerry was a much more experienced driver than she.

"You got here all right." He took his place in the front seat while she turned around to head for the highway. "Tell me what gives in Eastfield," he finally said. She couldn't see his face but he sounded tense and uncomfortable. He took a pack of cigarets from his jacket pocket, then put it back unopened.

Marge told him first of the activity at the woodshop. "Mr. Matthews may have another raft ready for me to take somewhere when we get there," she said.

"How do you know where to go?"

"I get instructions from the communications headquarters Shorty has set up."

"Is everybody working? The kids, I mean?" he asked.

"I guess everybody," Marge said. "Janey's at the medical clinic and the Digbee twins will work there too. Carol and

Lois are on the kitchen squad. Bill Tanner's with the auto corps." She hesitated, then went on. "That's where your father's working, too. They sent him to the dairy to see if he could get milk, when the trucks didn't come in."

Jerry just said "Oh."

When they got to the flood scene they found members of the emergency auto squad waiting to transport cold and hungry and sick victims of the disaster to the school or emergency clinic, and Dr. Tozian was among them. He sat alone in his car and greeted Marge and Jerry without a question when Marge stopped the station wagon near him.

"What about the McGoverns?" she called. He motioned to the raft, now being propelled to shore by two sturdy men. Huddled in the center were the two old people.

"The officers had a rough time with them," Dr. Tozian shouted above the wind. "They didn't know about Mr. McGovern's eyes and he slipped off the raft and nearly drowned. They had to drag him back into the house and get dry clothes on him before they could try it again. We need to get him to the clinic as soon as possible."

"Let us take them," Marge offered. "Maybe they'd be less frightened with someone they know."

"You're probably right," Dr. Tozian agreed. "I'll wait for the next load. People who are getting the broadcasts know where cars are waiting."

When the raft neared shore Jerry was out of the car and wading ankle deep in mud at the water's edge, followed by Dr. Tozian. Together they helped the aged couple ashore while Dr. Tozian carried the weeping woman to the station wagon. Jerry slipped his arms under Mr. McGovern's and with his own sure strength got the man to the car.

"It's me, Marge Ragland," Marge tried to comfort them as she held the car door open. "We'll have you safe in Eastfield in a few minutes. We'll take Mr. McGovern to the medical clinic in the town hall."

"Take him to the hospital in Andover," Mrs. McGovern

begged. "He has to go Monday for his operation. Take him now. I'll call our daughter from there."

Marge turned to Dr. Tozian questioningly.

"I think that's what you should do," he said as he put Mrs. McGovern in the back seat. "Our Eastfield hospital would just have to transfer him, anyway. They're full."

Jerry touched her elbow and she looked into a troubled face. There was no sneer now nor look of spite or self pity. The actual flood had been a shock and his expression was serious.

"Maybe I'd better drive this trip," he said. "You sit in back with her."

He took his place at the wheel beside Mr. McGovern, replacing the man's rain-sogged coat with his own dry jacket.

"These operations are nothing today," Marge heard him say. "My father's uncle had cataracts removed last fall. He's past eighty and sees fine now."

"That's what the doctor said," the farmer answered, through chattering teeth.

"As for your orchard, isn't water good for trees in the spring?"

Marge took Mrs. McGovern's hands in hers. Jerry had stuff, Rod had said. For the first time she believed it.

"But my home!" Mrs. McGovern wailed above the roar of the river and the rushing wind. "Everything downstairs is ruined and by night everything upstairs will be too. I'll never get things dried out, or that awful smell out of the house. All our furniture. Our new television. Henry should have sold the place to Judson Whiting last fall when he had the chance, instead of just giving an option."

"Sold? Gave an option?" Marge repeated. What did it mean? It was the explanation of what had taken place the night of the Harvest Hop, only she didn't understand it, and Mrs. McGovern didn't say any more. She would ask Rod when she had a chance. The thing to do now was get the farmer into the hospital and she was glad Jerry was at the wheel. Under his sure hand they could travel faster, and he knew the most direct route to the hospital, once in Andover.

"Wait in the car while I go in," he directed when they got there. "They may want to call your doctor, or get a wheel chair or something."

Mr. McGovern did not protest and his wife had stopped weeping. When Jerry returned he had assistance, and soon the McGoverns were well taken care of.

Marge got into the front seat but again Jerry drove. For a time he did not speak, and more than once he shook his head as though trying to drive some memory out of mind.

"I had no idea. Honestly, Marge, I had no idea," he said at last. "We had the radio on, but I guess I wasn't listening."

"I know," Marge said quietly. "I don't always listen to it, either."

He drove directly to Eastfield High School and in a few minutes he and another boy were loading a second raft in Marge's car. Then he hurried back to Mr. Matthew's woodshop. All day Marge drove from the scene of the disaster to the relief stations in town, sometimes carrying thermos jugs of hot coffee and sandwiches back to the rescue workers. Late in the afternoon an officer gave her new instructions.

"Drive to the newspaper office where that fellow has his ham station," he told her. "This walkie-talkie of mine has gone dead and I can't take the time to fuss with it. Tell him to have a bridge warning broadcast. The Andover-Eastfield bridge isn't safe any more. Emergency supplies from Andover City will have to come across by boat, as soon as we can get boats there."

Marge hurried to *The Clarion*. Rod was reading a page proof of the front page.

"Here it is," he said and avoided her eyes. The page was spread out on Shorty's table and in bold type the headline challenged Eastfield.

DO YOU WANT ANOTHER DISASTER NEXT YEAR?

"Then let the aldermen vote to reject the X-Ello offer. Turn down the chance for a dam to control spring floods. Reject the opportunity for an organized housing development to provide for Eastfield's growing population and encourage a Shacktown at our doorstep."

Marge read the words with surprise. Judson Whiting was one of the town's leading citizens who opposed the sale. She looked at Shorty inquiringly and her mind went back to the day when his first headline announced the X-Ello offer. Hadn't Rod hinted at something like this then? Why had Mr. Whiting wanted the McGovern land? Was that the Eastfield Shacktown he predicted now?

Shorty's face was grim and he was hollow-eyed from lack of sleep.

"*The Clarion's* going all out to force the sale," he told her. "It's my number one target now; a campaign I've orders to wage, with all stops out and no holds barred." He gave a tired sigh, picked up the page proof and disappeared into the composing room.

"Does this mean the paper isn't going to campaign for our school?" Marge asked Rod. "What about our campaign? I was counting on Shorty."

"I know," he said, "but Mr. Whiting said 'one campaign at a time' and he thinks the X-Ello sale is more important than anything else. Now is the time to push it."

She stood by the long, oak table trying to think it out, slowly realizing that her campaign had been abandoned by the newspaper. The powerful publisher was going to lock horns with the town's accepted rulers and concentrate on X-Ello.

There was no sense in asking Rod anything more. Perhaps he knew why; perhaps he didn't. No sense in asking him about the McGovern option, either. Where Shorty was involved, Rod's loyalty was steadfast and Shorty had his working orders now. She changed the subject.

"Jerry's helping Mr. Matthews build rafts," she said dully.

Rod took a step toward her. "He came back then? Or did his father make him?"

"I don't know whether his father found him or not," Marge

said. "I went and got him early this morning. He's been working all day."

"You!" Rod stared at her in amazement. "You went back to Shacktown? Alone?"

She nodded.

"You . . . shamed him into coming back? He must have liked that!"

His words were more like a reprimand than the commendation she had expected. For a few minutes they stood beside the table in silence.

"Shorty's put an item in about Jerry's breakfront representing us in the Regional Industrial Arts Awards, but it's buried on page three," Rod finally said. "He gave the school woodshop a lot of credit in his story about the flood. That's all there is on page one, the flood and Mr. Whiting's editorial."

"I guess that's the real news," Marge conceded. "I'm glad the school got some recognition. Well, I'm off for another raft. I'll see you."

He nodded. How did he really feel about her success in bringing Jerry back to Eastfield? Jerry would stay now, unless something more went wrong.

Marge closed the newspaper door behind her and went out into the rain again. Perhaps it was subsiding a little, but it would be weeks before the water could drain off in the area near the river bed. She drove slowly to the antiquated school that now was sheltering the flood victims. Through the fan-shaped span of vision cleared by her creaking windshield wiper, it looked its tired years.

Perhaps it was the only school she would ever have. In her mind's eye she saw Judson Whiting, the unsmiling brown eyes, the fringe of white hair between his ears and the high bald dome of his head. He might stir up enough force in Eastfield to bring about the X-Ello sale, but if the school must wait until the dam was built and the factory erected, she would never enjoy its advantages.

While she took the last raft to the State Police Marge

thought of the campaign she had waged all year, and the boys and girls who had helped her. There was nothing for her to fight with now except the school paper. How about the type Shorty had saved? An idea slowly formed in her mind as she waited for the officers to come in. With that type and the school paper she might do something!

A car drove up beside her and in the semi-darkness she recognized Dr. Tozian. She started from the station wagon but he stopped her with a wave of the hand.

"Turn on your headlights first," he called. "We can guide the rafts in that way. It's pretty bad out on the water. Hard for the men to see where they're going."

Marge switched on her lights, then in the warmth and security of the front seat of Dr. Tozian's car she told him of the campaign the newspaper was launching, and the single purpose Mr. Whiting had decided upon.

"We can't ask anything of Shorty. We can't expect Rod to try," she told him. "But I had an idea. Shorty has saved the type from all the 'School We Want' articles. I saw it. Why couldn't we print a special edition of our school paper with just those articles? Why couldn't we deliver a copy to every house in Eastfield just before the School Board meeting when they have to decide what to ask the taxpayers for?"

"Why not?" Dr. Tozian was immediately enthusiastic. "Maybe Shorty was going to re-run the series in *The Clarion*. He can't now, if what you've just told me is true. But we can do something. We'll go to Superintendent Griffin right away . . ." he stopped abruptly.

"Marge, when did you see that type?"

"Just yesterday."

"We've got to get it," Dr. Tozian said. "And right away, before Shorty throws it in. He has no reason to hold it longer, if Mr. Whiting won't let him use it."

There was an urgency in his voice that alarmed Marge. Shorty might indeed break up the type to re-use it. The articles were of no use to him now.

"Maybe we'd better go to *The Clarion* as soon as we get back to Eastfield," Marge suggested.

"That's what we'll do," Dr. Tozian agreed. "We'll get that type and then we'll talk to Superintendent Griffin."

While they waited for the officers they planned the campaign they still might wage.

"The Chamber of Commerce can put on a drive of some sort to raise money for the paper we'll need," Dr. Tozian said. "The boys in Mr. Matthews' printing class can run it off— enough copies for every house in Eastfield—and after school hours. No cost there."

"Rod will know how Eastfield is divided for the newspaper routes, so we won't miss a single house or store," Marge added. "He can organize the delivery routes. The Chamber of Commerce members can deliver our final 'School We Want' issue. We want our school now, Dr. Tozian, while we're still here. We don't want two shifts next year, and we can't wait for X-Ello to buy Dodd Park and build a dam."

"I'll feel better when we get that type," Dr. Tozian said. He peered through the misty windshield into the foggy night and the rolling water. "Here they come; two rafts at least."

Marge and Dr. Tozian drove back to Eastfield with the latest group of cold and frightened people. The school was less of a bedlam now than it had been in the morning. Mother had her Red Cross cap jauntily topping her wavy brown hair and she looked fresher than she had earlier in the day. She had set up a Receiving Desk in the main corridor where everyone was being registered by a Junior Red Cross worker. From the lunchroom came the tantalizing odor of chicken pot pie and a cheerful clatter of dishes. A radio in Superintendent Griffin's office had been hooked up to the school's intercom system and carried music and news bulletins and State Police instructions to all. Everything had been organized with Mother in control. For a moment Marge stood inconspicuously in the doorway, marveling at the order her mother had brought from the first grief and chaos. How proud Dad would be of Mother!

Dad! How would he feel when he finally knew all about Marge's part in the events of the last two days? She shuddered and drove the memory of Shacktown from her mind.

She wasn't needed here. Dr. Tozian was leaving his latest group of people at the Receiving Desk. She followed him quietly out of the building.

From the school they went at once to *The Clarion*, driving the short distance in Dr. Tozian's car. There was no real reason for alarm Marge told herself, yet she felt a growing nervousness with each passing moment. Suppose Shorty, in frustration and perhaps in anger, had disposed of the type when Judson Whiting had given him those orders?

It seemed to Marge that Dr. Tozian was being needlessly cautious as he drove down empty Main Street. She peered ahead toward *The Clarion* office. When they got there, it was completely dark.

CHAPTER XV

THE BLASTOFF

Dr. Tozian pulled the car to the curb and for a moment he and Marge stared at the newspaper office disconsolately.

"They could be in one of the restaurants around here," Dr. Tozian said. "We'd better look before driving out to where Shorty lives."

"Let's try the door," Marge suggested. "They could have fallen asleep."

The knob turned in her hand and she pushed the door open. Dr. Tozian followed her as she felt her way through the darkness of the front office to the swinging door. The radio in Shorty's "shack" had been turned low but it was still on. Marge found the light switch. The next second revealed Rod asleep on the table, Shorty groggily lifting his head from where it had sunk on the radio.

"Hello," he said, shaking the sleep from his eyes. "I guess I dropped off."

"You did," Dr. Tozian said kindly. "Are you going to stand by again tonight?"

At the sound of voices Rod wakened, pulled himself upright, and sat on the table, hands across his knees.

"I'll stand by until the State Police sign off," Shorty said. "They thought they had everybody in about half an hour ago. Why? What brings you here?"

Dr. Tozian did not hedge. "The type for the 'School We Want' articles. Marge thinks you've saved it. We were afraid you might kill it."

Shorty got to his feet and walked into his city room. Rod swung off the desk, his eyes on his uncle's thin face.

"So you've discovered it?" Shorty was looking past Dr. Tozian to Marge. "You probably figured out why I saved it, too."

"I thought you intended to help us get the school we want," Marge answered. "If you can't now, Dr. Tozian thinks we might do it through the school paper."

"But the type doesn't belong to the school," Rod broke in. "The school only paid to have it set." He looked inquiringly at Shorty.

"All we want is to borrow it—or rent it if that's necessary," Dr. Tozian said. "We can't afford to have all of those articles re-set. We'll return the type as soon as we've run off our own special issue."

"But Mr. Whiting?" Rod questioned his uncle.

Shorty stuffed his hands in his pockets and looked from Marge to Dr. Tozian. On the mantel shelf over his desk the French clock ticked rapidly and Marge's heart beat in time with it. If Shorty said no, their campaign was over!

At last he shrugged his shoulders. "You know where it is, Marge. Show Dr. Tozian and get it out of here."

"But Mr. Whiting . . ." Rod protested again.

"I'll explain when I have to," Shorty said to his nephew. "They asked to borrow it and I said yes. That's it!"

Rod did not offer to help carry the type to Dr. Tozian's car. When the instructor and Marge had made their last trip, carefully carrying the trays which they had first wrapped in old newspaper, Dr. Tozian raised a hand to Shorty. Then he spoke to Rod. "We'll have a Chamber of Commerce meeting Monday noon," he said. "I hope you can make it."

"I hope so," was Rod's noncommittal reply.

"Do you suppose Rod will help us?" Marge asked when they drove away from the newspaper office. "We'll need him to lay out the routes, so we don't miss anyone."

"Rod's loyalties seem to be torn most of the time," Dr. Tozian said. "First Jerry against the world. Now Shorty and the paper on one hand and you and the school on the other. But I think Shorty'll help him see things through."

Rod wasn't the only one with divided loyalties, Marge thought to herself. Rod and Jerry on one hand and her own father on the other. That was something she couldn't tell even Dr. Tozian.

He let her out at the school, admonishing her to say nothing to Janey or anyone until he had cleared with Superintendent Griffin. Once the superintendent had approved, she and Janey could begin working out the details and she could present the plan to the Chamber of Commerce Monday noon.

At the reception desk Marge learned that her father had managed to get home, and had come for Mother. An alternate was in charge of the night shift.

Marge left hurriedly. At home everyone was talking at once. Dad and Mother sat on the davenport, hand in hand. Janey was curled up in a big chair beside the radio which she had turned low. Marge looked at her father. His eyes were shining and he kept patting Mother's hand.

"I'm certainly proud of the Ragland women," he said. "The radio at the Capitol was praising you and your Red Cross every half hour! The work at the emergency clinic too, Janey." He smiled at his elder daughter then looked at Marge in the doorway. She knew how bedraggled she was, her rain hat pulled low, her blue rain coat and boots stained and mud spattered.

"You must have been working too, Marge," he said. "Get out of those rain togs and give us your report."

166

"Marge has been working since the first alert," Mother said, speaking for her. "She's been out with the station wagon all day."

"Doing what?" her father asked as she tugged at her rain boots in the hall.

"Getting rafts to the river for the State Police," Marge answered. "Getting people to the school from all sorts of places."

Like Shacktown, she thought to herself, with an inward shudder, remembering that she must tell him before long that she had been there with Jerry and Rod.

The telephone rang while Mother and Janey were still recounting experiences, some sad, some amusing. Dad answered it and came back with a puzzled expression on his face.

"It was Dr. Tozian. He said to tell you girls Superintendent Griffin had given you the green light. You and Janey can go ahead with your extra. What's this?"

"Yes, what is it, Marge?" Janey asked. "I haven't heard anything about it."

So Marge told about the position *The Clarion* had taken, and her own plan for an extra issue of the school paper with the type she and Dr. Tozian had saved.

Dad's face grew increasingly serious. "Somehow this Chamber of Commerce keeps getting embroiled, Marge," he said. "But if Superintendent Griffin thinks it's all right I guess you and Janey should be making your plans. I'll talk to Mr. Griffin later."

The idea of an extra edition of her paper appealed to Janey. "It's the big ending we were looking for," she said. "This year the school paper has really been significant. I'll have to write a strong introduction. Come on, let's get started."

The rain ended during the night and over the weekend evacuees were taken to the home of friends or placed with people who would provide board and shelter for the duration of the emergency. School would resume as usual on Monday.

It was Sunday afternoon before Marge had time to look up Carol and Lois. They were surveying their ruined flowers and shrubbery when she walked into their yard. The dank odor of the flooded river hung heavily over this section of Eastfield.

"Our bulbs are all washed out," Carol moaned. "Look at the forsythia bushes! Look at the hydrangea! Is it as bad up on Jewett Avenue where you live?"

"Our yard doesn't look quite as bad as this," Marge admitted. "Almost though."

"I think Mr. Whiting should pay for the replanting if we do the work," Lois chimed in. "I think Pops should try to make him!"

"Mr. Whiting?" Marge repeated. "Why Mr. Whiting?"

"He owns the place, we just rent," Carol explained. "He owns practically everything from here to Dodd Park. All the houses and the vacant lots too. The place where Shorty lives over on the next street. Everything, I guess."

So Mr. Whiting owned all the property from here to Dodd Park! He had an option on the McGovern farm too. For a moment Marge was speechless, then the pieces of the jig-saw puzzle began to form a pattern.

"Has he always owned it?" she asked.

"No, I don't think so," Carol said, kicking at a few rocks washed out of the edge of her flower bed. "Pops said he began buying up about a year ago. Pops thinks he knew all about the X-Ello offer before the company ever wrote to the mayor. They probably sounded out the newspaper first of all."

So that was the explanation! No wonder Mr. Whiting had let Shorty print his scoop before the aldermen met last fall. Probably Mr. Whiting himself had given Shorty the story. No wonder the editorial talked about an organized housing development. It would all have to be on Mr. Whiting's property. He even controlled the site for another Shacktown with the McGovern option! This was the reason Rod had hesitated to say he would help the Chamber of Commerce and the school paper with their latest plans. He knew Mr. Whiting didn't want to pay taxes for a new school on all this property. Mr. Whiting wanted to sell his lots and houses to the new X-Ello people before the school was built!

"What are you going to wear to the spring formal?" Carol chatted on. "I'm on the arrangements committee and I hope Lewis invites me. It would be awful to be on the arrangements committee and not have a date. Has Rod invited you yet?"

Rod hadn't asked her. If he had even thought about the spring formal, she didn't know it. She hadn't thought much about it herself until now.

"All I can think about is winding up our campaign for a new school," Marge answered. "That's what I came to talk to you about."

Carol and Lois were enthusiastic. They would certainly help.

Marge waited anxiously for social studies class Monday and the Chamber of Commerce meeting to follow. She was equally anxious to know whether Jerry had reported for school, and when Rod left the classroom as soon as the session was over, she followed him. He was headed for the woodworking shop again.

"Do you mind if I go too?" she asked.

Rod hesitated. "How is this going to make him feel?" he asked. "I haven't heard a thing from him."

"He knows I'll want to know whether he's going to stay in school," Marge replied.

"Okay, come along." Rod did not sound at all eager to have her.

The familiar skirr of saws and whine of drill presses sounded in the corridor. One by one the machines were turned off and the hum of voices supplanted the metallic medley. Marge and Rod stopped at the door. There, bending over the planks left over from the rafts was Jerry. Mr. Matthews was with him and two or three other boys crowded around. All looked up as Rod and Marge stepped inside.

"We're about to lock the barn door after the horse has been stolen," Mr. Matthews said. Jerry straightened up and grinned a hesitant greeting.

"Jerry thinks we can build a substantial rowboat with what's left over and some additional light weight lumber," Mr. Matthews explained.

"I have to think up some project to work on, now that my breakfront's finished and entered in the Regional," Jerry explained with a note of pride. He did not look at Rod and seemed to feel more at ease with his classmates than with his old friend. He had worked side by side with them during the emergency, Marge realized. When he last saw Rod it was in an unpleasant situation of Jerry's own making.

"A rowboat ought not to be difficult, after the project you've just finished," Marge spoke up. Without saying it, she wanted Rod to know there was no ill-feeling between herself and Jerry now.

Jerry looked at her quickly. "It'll keep me busy until the end of school, I guess," he said. Then he turned to the instructor. "It was swell of you and the fellows to crate my project and ship it. I guess—well, I'm not much good at making speeches. . . ."

The other boys seemed to understand. From the friendly grins and shoves as they took off their work aprons it was clear that Jerry was one of them. He seemed uncertain about facing his friend, though, until Rod spoke to him directly.

"What about lunch?" Rod asked. "Shall we go to the lunchroom here?"

Marge saw the bright response in Jerry's eyes. "I'll be right with you," he said and reached for the omnipresent comb to slick back his gleaming hair.

"What about the Chamber of Commerce meeting?" Marge asked. The boys weren't going to ask her to have lunch with them naturally, but wasn't Rod going to the meeting?

"I guess I'll skip it this time," he told her.

It was a disappointment, but she had expected it. The Digbee girls didn't come either. After it was over, she spoke to Dr. Tozian.

"What are we going to do if Rod doesn't show us how Eastfield is divided for the newspaper routes?"

"We'll get a map of the city and mark it off ourselves, the best we can," he said. "Don't push Rod. Mr. Matthews is counting on him to help keep Jerry in school. Maybe one thing at a time is all Rod can manage right now."

Tension and top drawer secrecy marked the production of the special issue of *Eastfield High School News*. Publication was timed for the Friday before the School Board was to meet and make its final decision. Should Eastfield taxpayers be asked to vote for an amount that would provide for the "School We Want"? The school paper asked everyone to call the School Board members and express an opinion.

Rod's attitude toward the project worried Marge and as he remained indifferent she felt hurt and abandoned. He had written one of the first articles, and had lined up most of the boys for her. Now he appeared alien, and resisted every attempt she or Dr. Tozian made to draw him into the undertaking. He dashed out of social studies for the woodshop each noon, and he and Jerry disappeared as regularly as before. Ruefully Marge remembered their jobs and the extra money they earned at Shacktown.

Not until the day before the printing was scheduled did Rod produce the map.

"Here it is," he said, passing a folder to Dr. Tozian. "The longest route is from College Row down to Jewett Avenue. It's the trickiest, too. I'll take that."

So he was going to stay with the school in the end! Marge wanted to say something to him, but he had avoided her for so long that she couldn't. She hoped he had planned to take that route so he could meet her in her own neighborhood after the school's rocket had been launched. She hadn't seen him alone, or walked his route with him in weeks. She wondered if by now Shorty had told Mr. Whiting about loaning the type for the school extra. If he hadn't, the publisher would soon know.

Like engineers at a space ship launching, the Chamber of Commerce group met at the high school early that Friday afternoon. Marge was sure Mr. Matthews himself had run off most of the papers in advance. The printing class couldn't have put them through the school's old hand press and assembled them in so short a time.

Marge watched the boys and girls arrive in groups of twos and threes. Carol and Lois had taken the places of the Digbee twins who hadn't attended the last few Chamber of Commerce meetings. Bill was there, ready to work with the others. Dr. Tozian handed each member his count of papers and the section of the map assigned.

Everybody was there except Rod!

She waited near Dr. Tozian's side, her eyes asking the question she was afraid to voice. The others were too busy with their maps, and reading the lead article Janey had written, to notice. Even Bill was reading it as though he had not seen it before.

"Do you mind coming back here after you've finished your route?" Dr. Tozian asked her quietly. "You have one of the shortest routes, and you've done it before."

She knew then that Dr. Tozian did not know where Rod was, and was worried too.

Marge hurried through her route, ringing doorbells and putting the "School We Want" issue into the hands of grown-ups whenever she could.

"Please read it and call at least one School Board member to let him know what *you* want," was the simple request the students made in the final step of their campaign.

If she was panting the words, she could not help it. She had to get through her route and back to school as quickly as possible. If Rod hadn't come, she would have to take his route now. College Row . . . Jewett Avenue . . . and Mrs. Brundage, who would challenge her again for meddling in civic affairs.

Both Dr. Tozian and Mr. Matthews were waiting at school when she returned.

"He hasn't come?" she asked. "Did you call Shorty?"

"Shorty isn't at *The Clarion*," Dr. Tozian told her. "Judson Whiting has sent him to one of the X-Ello plants in Indiana to get a feature story about the firm, and how it's accepted by a community where it's already operating."

"Jerry?" She was almost afraid to mention his name.

Mr. Matthews waved a telegram with an agitated gesture.

"The two boys left together, about the same time as always," he said. "And now I have this telegram. Jerry's breakfront has been advanced from the Regional to the Finals in Dearborn, Michigan. He's won one of the cash awards and now he may win the national scholarship. But where is he?"

CHAPTER XVI

STATE POLICE POST

Dr. Tozian drove Marge to the far end of her route on College Row. He didn't ask her any questions and she was grateful for that. If he knew where Rod and Jerry went each afternoon he might have discussed it with Mr. Matthews, but he did not mention it now.

"Good luck," he said as he let Marge out of the car. "Your campaign has a fighting chance, I'm sure."

Marge waved good-bye. Her campaign seemed less important now than the whereabouts of Rod and Jerry. What had kept Rod from taking his route?

It was peaceful up here on the hill in her father's world. Groups of students chatted on the campus, under the trees. Robins and orioles sang overhead. From the athletic field came the ring of bat against ball, and the cheers of students watching baseball practice. Faculty members were coming down the marble steps of the buildings where they taught. Soon Dad would leave the Administration Building. He would be home by the time Marge finished the route. A sense of dread came to her at the thought of her father. If only she had found a way to confide in him. She needed to talk to him now.

She reached Jewett Avenue at last and with a shudder rang Mrs. Brundage's bell. She wouldn't leave the paper with the maid. She would have to ask for Mrs. Brundage.

She thought her neighbor looked disturbed when she came to the front hall.

"I was sure somebody would be along soon," Mrs. Brundage said. "All right, give it to me. I just called your father and I'm on my way to see him now. We'll go together."

"But I have to finish the route," Marge protested. The last thing she wanted was to be questioned by Mrs. Brundage.

"There are only three houses between us," Mrs. Brundage reminded her. "Come along. You can tell me about the 'School We Want' on the way." She glanced at her reflection in the hall mirror—that straight hair-do, tailored blue silk suit, manicured nails. She always looked the same.

"It's all in the school paper," Marge told her. "All we are asking is that people read it, then call the School Board members."

"That's what I understand." Somebody had reported to her, of course.

When they reached home Dad was waiting at the door, pipe in hand. He motioned Mrs. Brundage to his study, took one of the papers from Marge, and prodded her along.

"Is there something serious about this?" he asked, glancing at the paper. "The girls told me they were reprinting the articles from the school paper just as they had appeared during the year. We've all seen them before now."

"It isn't just this political campaign your daughters have been running," Mrs. Brundage said coldly. "Do you know that two of the boys who've helped them engineer it are now in the custody of the State Police?"

"What?" Dad and Marge gasped the word simultaneously.

The State Police! Marge felt her cheeks burn as Mrs. Brundage fairly hurled the words, with their humiliating connotation, at them.

"The officers called my brother to see whether he would recommend releasing them when they couldn't get in touch with Mr. Chamberlin. It seems Mrs. Clarke was trying to watch both his shop and hers while he went somewhere for stock he needed. Andover, probably. Of course, Alexander couldn't take that responsibility."

"It's the boy Jerome, then," Dad assumed at once. "Jerome and who else?"

"The newspaper man's nephew whom I've seen Marge with a lot this past year!"

Dad's desk with its papers and books swayed before Marge's eyes. Rod held by the State Police! This was the trouble he had warned Jerry about. Marge had hoped, when Jerry came back to help during the flood and then remained in school, that he would give up Morris' vicious business, but the car and the money had been too appealing. He had only come back half way, and now he and Rod were both in real trouble. But Rod had nothing to do with Jerry's affairs at Shacktown!

Dad put his pipe aside and motioned everyone to chairs. "Marge, tell me what you know about this," he said. "Do you know why the State Police are holding the boys?"

"I can tell you," Mrs. Brundage said, seating herself in a chair Dad had moved in her direction.

"I want to hear what Marge has to say," he said. "She and Rod have been friends. I didn't know Jerome had any part in the school campaign. From what I'd heard the girls say, I thought he hadn't been part of any school activities."

"Up to the flood, he wasn't," Marge told her father. "He pitched in then and helped Mr. Matthews and the other wood-shop boys. But there aren't many jobs for kids in Eastfield after school except delivering papers, and all the routes are taken. At school the kids didn't take to Jerry at first. Nobody did except Rod, who had a special reason. So Jerry found some-place else to go and something else to do."

176

Mrs. Brundage gave a knowing "u-m-m-m-m," but didn't interrupt again. She knew where Jerry had been going all right. The State Police had told Mr. Dodd.

"All right, he had to do something," Dad conceded. "What has he been doing?"

She had to answer him. She wished Mrs. Brundage wasn't there, but in a way the presence of the arch enemy of her whole campaign stiffened Marge's determination to stand her ground. She would tell them everything she knew and defend the boys as best she could.

"Jerry's been selling beer at the bowling alley in Shacktown, in order to keep a hot-rod he bought," Marge said. "Rod's been earning a little money there by setting up pins. Rod had nothing to do with the beer business. He never rode in the car when Jerry had beer, but he knew about it and kept trying to influence Jerry to give it up and stay in school. Jerry's not been a truant, and he's kept his grades up."

"Have you known all this?" Dad asked. Marge had never seen his face so cold and severe. If she had only told him earlier! But how could she without getting the boys into trouble? They were in trouble now, and nothing was to be gained by keeping anything from her father any longer.

"I've only known it since the day before the flood," Marge said. "Jerry took his spite out on me because he knew I didn't like to have Rod running around with him. He drove us both out to the Shacktown bowling alley that afternoon, and the State Police searched the place while we were there. He didn't have any beer in the car and there wasn't anything they could do!"

Dad suppressed a groan and walked to the window. "Marge! Shacktown!"

"It's nothing but kids bowling," Marge told him. "The manager never lets them drink on the premises."

Mrs. Brundage could restrain herself no longer. "So this Jerome brings beer in from Andover City and sells it just off the premises," she said. "They caught him in the act this time."

177

"Marge, you could have been along," Dad said without looking at either her or Mrs. Brundage.

"No, I would never have gone with Jerry again," Marge said. "Not unless Rod made him quit. I didn't know what he was doing until that day."

She didn't think her father was listening. He stood with his back toward the room looking off in the direction of the college. Marge knew what must be going through his mind. Suppose she had been along this time.

What was Dad going to do? Rod and Jerry were being held by the State Police and who was there to help them with Shorty gone? The officers couldn't locate Mr. Chamberlin, either, and Alexander Dodd hadn't been willing to do anything. What was going to happen to the boys?

She spoke at last. "Dad, what are you going to do? Somebody's got to help them. Rod hasn't done anything but be friends with Jerry and try to keep him in school. Today Jerry's entry in the Industrial Arts Awards was advanced to the National Contest. He has a chance to win a scholarship and he doesn't even know it. If the State Police send him to jail or something, what is it going to mean to him? Shorty can't help them. Mr. Whiting's sent him to Indiana to get an X-Ello story."

"So you're doing battle for Jerome now?" Mrs. Brundage asked.

"For him and all the other kids who haven't a chance here in Eastfield," Marge defied her. "Not much chance for jobs and nothing to do. For me too, because we haven't got what I want, either. You must have read the articles we've printed in our school paper all year. You know what I want, and what the others want!"

Dad turned from the window. "Come on," he said. "Let's see this thing through."

Mrs. Brundage held back. "You aren't taking your daughter to the State Police Post?" she asked. The idea plainly was incredible to her.

"Why not?" Dad asked. "She's been to the Shacktown bowling alley—a place I've never seen. Why not? I think we should all know what it means to be held by the police."

He took Mrs. Brundage by the arm and gently urged her out of the back door and into the garage. From the kitchen window Marge saw her mother watch them drive away in the old station wagon. How much did Mother know? What had she heard through the open door of Dad's study?

No one spoke on the ride to the Police Station. The asphalt glistened in the afternoon sunshine. Green branches of trees arched overhead, their shadows a moving pattern on the highway. In the fields that slipped past, cattle meandered slowly toward big barns. Red-winged blackbirds chirped on fence posts. But in this peaceful world there was trouble, and for Rod and Jerome it was serious trouble. Was Dad going to help them or just teach Marge a lesson?

He swung the car off the highway onto a gravel entrance. This was it—the State Police Post half way between Eastfield and Andover City. She had seen it, but at the same time had never seen it before; a small white stucco building, square and plain without a tree around it. Large windows gave a view in all directions. At the rear was a garage and through the open doors Marge could see two cars and two motorcycles.

Silently Dad led the way into a big, bare room, its dull green walls reminding Marge of the corridors at school. A wooden bench and several plain chairs lined the walls. Behind the one dark oak desk an officer in uniform looked at them inquiringly, waiting for them to make their errand known. A second man turned the radio down as Dad introduced himself and Mrs. Brundage, then busied himself at file cases back of the desk and appeared uninterested.

"I understand you have two Eastfield boys here," Dad said. "Could we see them?"

"We had to put them in the bull pen," the officer in charge half apologized. "No place out here for juveniles, but that's all right.We aren't holding any criminals right now. We're expecting a Mr. Chamberlin. Some neighbor of his said she'd have him come the minute he got back to his store."

Marge stared at a big calendar over the officer's desk while he opened a drawer and took out a ring of clanking keys. The sound sent a chill through her.

"This way," the man said and motioned to a stairway at the back of the room. Once more Mrs. Brundage held back, and once more Dad took her arm and propelled her forward. The bare stairs creaked under their feet as they went up. The scent of a strong disinfectant permeated the long hall which divided the second floor.

Five cells lined one wall, each with an iron grill door, double decker cot, wash bowl and toilet, and iron grills over the window. What lay beyond the opposite wall Marge could only guess. Some sort of living quarters for the officers, perhaps.

She saw Rod and Jerry at once, sitting side by side on the cot in the farthest cell, and she hurried ahead of Mrs. Brundage to follow her father to their door, but when she got there she could think of nothing to say but a cheerless "hello." Never had she expected to see Rod behind cold, black bars. Why were they holding Rod? Could he possibly have been helping Jerry this time? She refused to believe it.

At the sight of their visitors Rod, misery on every feature, got to his feet. Jerry turned his face toward the window.

"Rod. . . ." Marge knew her voice was questioning him. There had to be an explanation.

"Marge, you shouldn't have come here," he said. "Or brought anyone else here."

She clutched at the bars of the door. "Of course we came," she said hoarsely. "We know Shorty's in Indiana."

Jerry got to his feet then. "Rod didn't need to stay here," he said but he avoided their eyes. "Rod didn't do anything. They told him he could go."

"That's right," the officer said. "Rod can go any time. Staying here was his idea."

"You see," Marge turned to face her father and Mrs.

Brundage. "I knew Rod hadn't done anything. He was only trying . . ." She choked and could find no words to go on which would not crush Jerry even more.

"Only trying to help me," Jerry finished for her. "I don't mind your saying it. If I'd listened to him we wouldn't be here, either of us."

He stuffed his hands into the pockets of his slacks and turned to look through the barred windows to the fields outside.

"But now . . ." Marge hesitated. "You're through with Morris now, aren't you?"

"What do you think?" he asked bitterly. "How stupid could I be?" He still did not look at her, and Rod stood in wretched silence watching him.

"Maybe you two had better go back down stairs and wait for me," Dad said. "I'll talk to the boys and the officer alone."

Marge touched his arm. "You'll help them?" she pleaded. "Somebody's got to help them. They're . . . my friends."

Through an unsteady mist she looked into the bare cell that held the two boys. Jerry's startled, black eyes were looking at her intently. His lips moved but he couldn't speak. Rod's hand reached toward her, then fell to his side. She felt Mrs. Brundage's hand on her shoulder, turning her back toward the stairs.

"Come," she said and the coldness had left her voice. "He'll help them."

Mrs. Brundage followed close behind Marge, fumbling in her big alligator bag for something. Then they waited in the bare room below for an endless time. Marge counted the pine floor boards, the spokes in the worn chairs, listened to the officer pick out a report on the typewriter with the slow two-finger hunt-and-peck system. She was accustomed to her father's pipe, but the cigar smoke in the room was heavy and almost nauseating. At last Dad came down, followed by Rod and the officer.

"Jerry?" Marge asked at once. "What are they going to do about Jerry?"

"He's going to wait until his father comes," Dad said. "They would have released him to me but he prefers to wait for his father."

So it was Dad who had influenced Jerry to get things straight with his father.

Marge thought quickly. "Dad, please call Mr. Matthews and make sure he finds a way to let Mr. Chamberlin know about the Industrial Arts Award Jerry's just won," she urged. "Mr. Matthews might not have called him. Mr. Chamberlin has one reason for being proud of Jerry. Jerry doesn't know about it unless you told him."

"Jerry won!" Rod exclaimed. "He really won? I knew he would!"

Dad nodded. "I didn't tell Jerry, and you're right, Marge. His father needs to know, and be the one to tell him."

The officer indicated the telephone. "Right here, Dr. Ragland," he said.

"Why don't you two wait in the car," Mrs. Brundage suggested. "I'll stay here with your father, Marge."

The officer waved a hand toward the door and Marge and Rod left the prison-plain room for the freedom and fresh air of the yard. They got into the back seat of the wagon and waited side by side for Dad and Mrs. Brundage.

"You were swell," Rod said, taking Marge's hand. "Jerry didn't want to see his father at first. You know how they haven't hit it off. Jerry didn't want the officers to call his father, but they tried to get him, of course. Then you came—and this was the second time. When you said he was your friend . . . and the way your father talked to him, just as though Jerry was his boy . . ." Rod hesitated. "I didn't really know your father until now, Marge. I guess I was a little afraid of him."

It was good to hear Rod praise her father. Marge smiled at Rod. "Jerry won't sell any more beer, will he?" she asked. "And he'll stay in school, won't he? They won't keep him . . . here or somewhere?"

"I don't think so," Rod said. "They would have released him to your dad if Jerry hadn't decided his own father should be responsible. And he'd already promised to stay in school. You know how he felt when he found out Mr. Matthews and the boys had crated his breakfront and entered it for him."

Marge remembered that day, and how good she and Rod had felt.

"And now he's won an award!" Rod went on. "Well, we've both had enough of Shacktown now, but what we're going to do about jobs and money I don't know."

"Jerry can always help his dad at the radio shop, and business may get better for them," Marge said. "You've got your job at *The Clarion*."

"Maybe!" Rod sounded grim. "Do you realize what time it is? This is the second time I've failed to show up and count out for the boys. If Shorty didn't get back from Indiana in time to take over for me, what do you suppose happened in the alley back of the pressroom this afternoon? What do you think Mr. Whiting's going to say?"

CHAPTER XVII

A CHANCE FOR THE "WORLD WE WANT"

MARGE HADN'T THOUGHT of the hour nor who was counting out for Rod today. True, it was the second time he had failed to appear and take charge of the newsboys. If Shorty wasn't there—and he couldn't be or he would have called the State Police—who had done what?

Marge could envision the papers running off the moving belt and piling up on the rough brick paving in the alley. Chaos was what her mind's eye conjured up. Piles of scrambled newspapers and panicked newsboys not knowing what to do.

But would the pressman have started the run again without making certain Rod or someone was there? He had done that once before, and she was the one who had averted confusion. What would he have done? Gone to Mr. Whiting for instructions? Marge felt her throat grow tight and dry at the thought. Rod had nothing to say when she looked at him.

"The officer said you could have gone at any time," Marge

reminded him. "Couldn't you have left Jerry when it got this late? He would have understood."

He nodded. "I kept thinking every minute that we'd get a call from Shorty," he explained. "They left word for him to call. Then when it got to the time when I should go, we were locked up in the last cell on the second floor and no way to talk to the officers. Maybe if we'd screamed and rattled the bars they would have heard us. That's what we were talking about when you and the rest of them came."

And when they had come there was all that waiting and talking, Marge remembered. Now here she and Rod sat while Dad and Mrs. Brundage were still with the officers. It was too late to do anything about it now, anyway; whatever had happened was over with!

Dad and Mrs. Brundage came out at last and got into the front seat. Soon the State Police Post disappeared behind them, the road ahead was straight and tree-shaded, and the scent of clover came from the fragrant fields that reached toward home.

Marge leaned forward in her seat. "Dad, when we get to Eastfield, would you take Rod and me to *The Clarion*? If Shorty didn't get there in time to take care of Rod's job for him, we don't know who counted out."

"Counted out?" Mrs. Brundage repeated, turning in the front seat to look back at them, a puzzled expression on her face.

"For the newsboys," Rod explained. "Somebody has to give them the right number of papers. If Shorty didn't get there . . . I don't know . . . Mr. Whiting . . ."

"Mr. Whiting! Humph!" Mrs. Brundage sounded disgusted. "I'd like to see Mr. Whiting count them out himself!"

It seemed to Marge that her father suppressed a chuckle. She tried to picture fat, balding, jowly Mr. Whiting counting out papers in the alley. It was too incongruous. Fleetingly she wondered if Mrs. Brundage knew why Mr. Whiting wanted the X-Ello sale approved before the School Board built an enlarged and improved school. Of course she did! Alexander Dodd and Mrs. Brundage knew everything in Eastfield!

None of that mattered so much now. Again Marge leaned forward to talk to her father.

"Probably Mr. Whiting's not going to like that extra issue we got out at school, after he decided to campaign for only the X-Ello sale," she went on. "We're afraid he's going to be furious with Shorty for loaning the type, and now with Rod for not being on the job. Rod's going to need that job worse than ever. . . ." She didn't need to explain there would be no more income from the bowling alley in Shacktown. Dad knew that.

"Mr. Whiting'll win the X-Ello battle," Mrs. Brundage conceded. "I don't know what you youngsters can do about getting him to campaign for this 'School We Want' business though." She didn't sound at all antagonistic and as she turned back in her seat her next words surprised Marge completely.

"Dr. Ragland, if instead of calling some School Board member who already knows where you stand on the question of improved schools, suppose you were to write an open 'Letter to the Editor.' He'd have to print it. He couldn't ignore you."

"I'm afraid he could," Dad said, "but if enough solid citizens came out openly in support of our children's campaign, he'd have to think twice. Then the School Board could act more courageously. The students have certainly done their part as young citizens."

Rod and Marge looked at each other in silence. Dad *was* in favor of improved schools, but what had he said to Mrs. Brundage back in the State Police Post? Or had the sight of Rod and Jerome, forlorn on a hard cot in a police cell, changed her attitude? She wasn't arguing or disagreeing with Dad now. She didn't say she would write a letter. Probably she would have to talk to Alexander Dodd before she changed her position openly, but Marge felt convinced that Mrs. Brundage would not take a stand against them. Wasn't she just now suggesting a way in which Dad could help?

Dad increased his speed. "We'll get you there as fast as we can, Rod," he said. "You want to help him with his route I take it, Marge."

He drove them directly to *The Clarion* and let them out at the front door. The girl behind the front office counter was putting on her hat and she looked at them dubiously but said nothing. Marge followed Rod into the city room. Stacked on Shorty's long table was a pile of papers—too many to be Rod's own downtown route. Just beyond, his back to them and fists clenched at his sides, stood Shorty, facing Judson Whiting.

"So our papers are more than an hour late in getting out!" The words came from deep in Shorty's throat. "The voters up on College Hill won't be able to read our latest exhortation to sell to X-Ello until after dinner tonight! But what about our kids, picked up by the State Police? Juvenile delinquents now! What about that? And who's to blame? Eastfield and its controlling citizens!"

Neither Rod nor Marge could speak. They stared in amazement from Shorty to the belligerent newspaper owner towering above him, one hand gripping the back of a chair. A massive ring glistened on his fat little finger. Marge's eyes traveled upward from his immaculate, well-tailored tweed suit to his red and perspiring face. Mr. Whiting, domineering, pompous, fierce in his wrath, would make any less powerful man tremble, but Shorty was standing up to him. Mr. Whiting wasn't answering Shorty, either, and in the frightening silence of the city room, the racing French clock ticked loudly.

"I'll deliver the papers on this last route myself if Rod doesn't get here soon, and Tim doesn't want to take two," Shorty went on. "They've released Rod. That's all I know."

"I'm here," Rod broke in and for the first time Mr. Whiting's cold eyes turned from Shorty. Shorty, too, wheeled to face them in the doorway. The bitter lines in his face disappeared when he saw his nephew and Marge.

"How did you get here?" he asked.

"Dr. Ragland brought me."

"Dr. Ragland!" Mr. Whiting spoke for the first time. Marge felt his eyes on her, saw the astonishment in his face.

"There wasn't anyone else to go for them," Marge explained. "Shorty wasn't back from Indiana and they couldn't locate Mr. Chamberlin. So Dad took Mrs. Brundage and me and we went for them."

"Mrs. Brundage!" The publisher almost gasped the name. Two of the most influential people in Eastfield had gone to the State Police Post for Rod and Jerome while Mr. Whiting was storming in wrath because his papers were delivered late. The full significance of it came to Marge when she glanced down at a crumpled paper on the floor at his feet. It was her paper, the "School We Want" extra. Undoubtedly that had added to his fury. Shorty would have to admit he had kept the type and loaned it to the School Journalism Club, but in his present indignation Marge knew Shorty would have stood his ground on that decision too.

When Mr. Whiting spoke again his voice was controlled and he was completely calm. He might have been fierce with Shorty, even undignified, but in front of Marge and Rod he was lordly and superior.

"Dr. Ragland and Mrs. Brundage know all about this paper of yours?" he asked, glancing momentarily at the crumpled extra.

"Oh yes," Marge told him. "I think my father is going to send you a 'Letter to the Editor' about it instead of just phoning a School Board member. Rod and Jerry would never have been in Shacktown at all if we'd had the school we need and things to do and ways to earn money here at home."

Marge saw the look of triumph on Shorty's face and breathed easier. Shorty must think, as Mrs. Brundage had suggested, that Judson Whiting would not refuse to print a letter her father wrote. Perhaps Shorty was glad she, too, had dared to speak up to Mr. Whiting.

Shorty turned his attention to Rod again. "Look, these are Tim's papers. He did the best he could to count out for the other boys and he took your downtown route so the papers would be in the stores before they close. Now you take his route—College Row down to Jewett Avenue. You know it. You may be fired when you get back, but take Tim's papers and deliver them!"

Mr. Whiting watched Rod reach for the papers. "Use your own judgment about that, Shorty," he said, "but if Dr. Ragland writes a 'Letter to the Editor' see that it gets at the top of the Editorial page."

With no nod or further word to any of them, he walked through Shorty's "shack" to his own office.

"I guess he was pretty mad," Rod said in a quiet voice as he packed the papers in the canvas bag that lay in a heap beside them.

"So was I when I found out what you boys have been up to," Shorty said, but he didn't sound mad. "We'll talk about that later. Now I'll drive you up to College Row and you can get started. You're late enough."

So for the second time that day Marge followed the route that led from the green, landscaped college campus past the comfortable faculty homes with their wide yards and flowers and shrubs, down to Jewett Avenue, but Rod was with her this time.

"Marge, do you suppose your father really will write a 'Letter to the Editor?'" he asked. "You heard what Mr. Whiting said."

"I think he will. I'll talk to him about it," she said. She would, too. Perhaps it was her fault that Dad hadn't talked to her more, and sometimes seemed to mistrust her judgment. She had always gone to Mother with everything, instead of to Dad. It was Janey who went to Dad.

"I'll talk to him, Rod, and if he says he will, there's one more thing we can do. I've just thought of it."

"What's that?" he asked.

"All the kids who wrote the articles for the school paper can get their parents to write 'Letters to the Editor' too!"

Rod whistled softly. "If Jerry wins that scholarship, Shorty'll play that up, just as he gave credit to the woodworking boys at the time of the flood! That proved what a school can do for a town like Eastfield! Why, we'll have *The Clarion* campaigning for us even if the publisher is against us! That's a real nuclear idea! What a girl!" He reached for her hand and held it tightly. "You are my girl, aren't you? I never really had a girl, but now . . ."

She stepped closer to his side and smiled her answer. She was really his girl at last. There wouldn't be any more misunderstandings over Jerry or Shacktown or anything else, and together they'd win their campaign.

Wisconsin State College at Eau Claire
LIBRARY RULES

No book should be taken from the Library until it has been properly charged out by the librarian.

Books may be kept two weeks, and renewed for one additional week.

A fine of ten cents a day will be charged for books kept over time.

In case of loss or damage the person borrowing this book will be held responsible for a part or the whole of the value of a new book plus processing costs.

DUE	DUE	DUE	DUE
Mar 2 64	JUL 29 '66	FEB 27 '68	
Mar 10	OCT 3 66	MAR 20 '68	
Mar 31	99. 9 100	MAY 6 '68	
MAY 5 '64	JAN 9 '67	JUL 15 '68	
SEP 25 '64		DEC 2 '68	
OCT 27 '64	JAN 9 '68		
NOV 24 64	MAR 3 '67		
		FEB 19 68	
JAN 28 '65	MAY 10 '67	FEB 21 '68	
MAY 25 '65		MAR 10 69	
SEP 23 '65			
	OCT 30 '67	APR 21 '69	
NOV 3 '65	DEC 1 '67	APR 23 '70	
JAN 17 '66	JAN 31 '68	SEP 23 '71	
MAY 4 '66	FEB 8 '68	OCT 12 '71	
MAR 24 '66			